Available Titles from Frontier 2000 Media

Non Fiction:

No Regrets: How Homeschooling Earned me a Master's Degree at Age Sixteen

Writing for Today

Looking Backward: My Twenty-Five Years as a Homeschooling Mother

Adult Fiction:

The Fourth Kingdom

The Twelfth Juror

The Warrior

Children's Fiction:

Tales of Pig Isle

The McAloons: A Horse Called Lightning & A House of Clowns

Scripture references from *The Living Bible*, copyright ©1971 are used by
permission of Tyndale House Publishers, Inc. Wheaton, IL 60189. All
Rights Reserved.

ISBN-13 978-1477425169
ISBN-10 1477425160

Dedication

To the millions of women who are changing the world, one prayer at a time.

The Warrior

Joyce Swann

Chapter 1

Elizabeth Anderson was behind the wheel of her Honda Pilot speeding toward the airport. She knew that she was driving too fast, but she couldn't seem to help herself. It was growing dark, and by the time she reached downtown Ft. Worth night had set in. Elizabeth knew that she should slow down, but that was out of the question; she had to get to the airport.

Suddenly, in her headlights she saw a young man standing in the street with a crushed motorcycle at his feet. Elizabeth braked and managed to slow her SUV, but she was unable to stop. As she passed, the young man looked at her and grew filmy, as if he were making a transition from life to death. Horrified, she extended her hand and shouted twice, "Don't die if you don't know Jesus!" With great effort she turned the SUV around and headed back to the scene of the accident.

Elizabeth's eyes flew open. She was lying on her side staring at the clock on her bedside table. It was 5:03 A.M. Her heart was pounding wildly, and her pink silk pajamas lay cold and smooth against her skin. She reached out to touch her husband Boomer who was asleep beside her. She wanted to wake him and tell him every detail of her nightmare, but she decided against it. Boomer had to get up at 6:00 to get ready for work; if she woke him now, he would probably not be able to go back to sleep.

Wide awake and still feeling the effects of her nightmare, Elizabeth slipped out of bed and tiptoed down the stairs. When she reached the main floor, she went into the large comfortable library. She sat down in Boomer's big vintage leather chair that had belonged to his grandfather and pulled her bare feet up under her. Whenever she felt upset or scared or generally out of control, Elizabeth sat in Boomer's chair. The chair was like him: big, warm, comfortable, and she always felt calm there. More than any other room in the house, the library was a reflection of Boomer. The honey colored salvaged heart pine that covered the walls and the massive fireplace with its gently arched opening created a feeling of strength without seeming overbearing. This was Elizabeth's safe place.

Elizabeth knew that she would not be able to go back to sleep, and she wondered what she should do for the next hour or so before Boomer and the girls got up. As she sat thinking about the day ahead of her, however, she could not quite push the dream out of her mind. The more she tried, the more she felt that she needed to pray for the young man. The very idea seemed foolish, but she could not help believing that the Holy Spirit was leading her to pray.

At 5:16 Elizabeth yielded to that urgency. Bowing her head and stretching out her hands palms up, she began praying aloud, "Dear Jesus, I don't know whether a young man was in an accident tonight, but you do. I believe that if someone were in an accident, you sent me that dream so that I would pray for him. So, Jesus, if he is real, I'm asking you to take care of that young man. Please, Lord, don't let him die. Heal him, and if he doesn't know you, surround him with Christians who love you more than anything in the world and who will tell him about you. Dear Jesus, please save him and help him to become the man you created him to be. Amen."

After Elizabeth had finished praying, she felt certain that the young man in her dream did exist and that God had arranged for her to pray for him. As she headed for the kitchen to put on the coffee, she smiled and said, "Thank you, Jesus."

Chapter 2

$\mathcal{M}$anny Rodriguez and his crew arrived on the scene at 5:11 A.M. The intersection of Jordan and Archer was one of the busiest in Ft. Worth during rush hours. By 7:00 A.M. it would be a traffic nightmare, but at this time of morning the streets were nearly deserted. The Denny's Restaurant on the corner to his right had a half dozen patrons—travelers no doubt. The Shell station on the corner to his left had not yet opened for the day's business, and the strip mall behind him would not open until 10:00 A.M. He wondered whether the police would be able to locate any witnesses.

Manny had bigger problems, however. The twisted metal of a motorcycle lay in the center of the intersection, but no rider was in sight. "Spread out, guys!" Manny shouted. "Whoever was riding this bike has to be around here somewhere."

In less than a minute Mark Horner, the youngest member of the crew, called out, "Rodriguez! He's over here!"

Manny began to run toward the median where Mark Horner was standing. Even in the dim light, he could tell

Joyce Swann

from the expression on Mark's face that it was not good. Then he saw the body. He was just a kid, approximately the same age as Manny Jr. Manny felt his heart leap. He could imagine the horror that this kid's parents would feel when the police arrived at their door to tell them that their son was dead—because he certainly was dead. Manny had been a first responder for twenty years, and he knew a dead person when he saw one.

Manny was also a professional. He would do everything possible to resuscitate this kid; he would begin CPR, transport him, and leave it to the doctors at the hospital to pronounce him DOA. Manny bent over to begin his work while Mark ran to bring the ambulance around and alert the rest of the crew.

To Manny's astonishment, the kid moved his head and said, "Help me, man."

Manny quickly regained his composure and responded as casually as he could, "That's why I'm here. You had a little accident. You're not hurt very bad, but we gotta take you to the hospital. Can you tell me your name?"

"James Goodwin."

"Well, James, I'm going to give you some oxygen. You don't really need it, but it'll help you feel better." As Manny continued to chat in an almost casual manner, he worked with a speed and efficiency that would have signaled to an observer that the young man's condition was far more serious than Manny was willing to let him know.

When James had been loaded into the ambulance, Manny sat next to him and began talking. "Okay, James, we're gonna turn on the siren. We don't need to hurry to the

~ 6 ~

hospital because you're not hurt very bad, but traffic is getting heavy and I want to get everybody out of our way. Now, tell me what happened."

As the siren blared and the ambulance sped through the streets, James told Manny everything he could remember. "I was visiting my mom and dad for a few days and left this morning to go back to Angel Fire where I live. I was sitting at the red light when I heard a noise behind me, like a really loud engine. I looked around and saw a pick-up coming like really fast, man, but I didn't have time to move. I knew it was going to hit me, but I couldn't get out of the way. The next thing I remember is seeing you standing over me. "

"Where's Angel Fire?"

"New Mexico."

"I've never heard of Angel Fire. Is it a nice place?"

"It's awesome. You should come there to ski."

"They have good skiing there?"

"It's totally rad."

"Do you ski, James?"

"I dunno."

"Okay, James. That's good. What else happened?"

"Nothing. I'm tired. I'm going to sleep."

"No, wait. " Manny responded. "I didn't understand what you said about the accident. Tell me again what happened."

James was very tired. He was warm and comfortable and was not feeling any pain. Talking took so much effort that he could hardly speak, and when he did, his voice shook. "I already told you everything."

"I need you to tell me again. It's important because I gotta fill out a report. Tell me what happened."

James repeated his story almost verbatim. When he finished, Manny asked him for his parents' address and phone number. It was important to keep James talking; if he went to sleep, he wasn't going to wake up.

Chapter 3

*A*fter Boomer left for work, Elizabeth drove the girls to school. Molly was two weeks away from her seventeenth birthday, and Tracy was fifteen. Elizabeth watched them walk up the steps and enter the building before she drove away. They looked very much like her except that they were taller; they had Boomer to thank for their long legs. They were, however, very different in their personalities—Tracy was sweet and gentle, and Molly was funny and witty. Elizabeth could not look at them without feeling her heart grow warm.

Elizabeth pulled her Pilot back into the traffic. She would go to the women's Bible study at her church and afterwards drive to the mall to buy a gift for Boomer. Wednesday would be their twenty-fifth wedding anniversary, and Boomer's birthday was two days later. She needed to find something special enough to cover both occasions.

As she drove through the familiar streets, Elizabeth's thoughts drifted back to the first time she had seen Boomer. She was a freshman at Stephen F. Austin High School in Garland and he was a senior. She thought that he was the most handsome guy in the school and quickly developed a huge crush on him, but he never knew that she was there. It wasn't that he chose to ignore her; he was simply unaware that she existed.

Boomer Anderson was a pretty good student and a pretty good athlete. His position on the football team, along with his friendly personality and good looks, earned him a certain amount of popularity. His Christianity earned him a certain amount of disdain. He participated in many school activities, but he was often excluded from the private parties because he had a reputation for being something of a goody-goody.

Boomer's father owned half a dozen hardware stores in and around Garland, and this gave Boomer the status of a "rich kid" among his peers. Although his father made more money than almost anyone Boomer knew, he never thought of himself as rich. He had always spent weekends and summers helping his dad at the stores, and he had learned the value of hard work while he was still very young.

After Boomer's high school graduation, he moved to Dallas to attend SMU and earn a degree in architecture. He had always been involved in the remodeling of the stores, and he discovered early on that he loved anything connected to building and design. Before his first semester ended, Boomer knew that he had made the right choice.

By the time Boomer had earned his degree he had landed a job with Dungee, Harris, and Schmidt, one of the most respected architectural firms in Dallas. He would not begin until September so he decided to spend the summer in Garland helping his dad at the stores. "It's funny," he thought, "I'm now officially an architect, and I'm still selling nuts and bolts."

A week after his return to Garland, Boomer was working at the Dyer Street store when Elizabeth walked through the door. Her mother had sent her to buy a washer for the dripping kitchen faucet, and she had no idea how to find one that would fit. Although she recognized Boomer immediately, as far as he was concerned, it was the first time he had ever seen her. She was small and curvy and completely feminine, and by the time she had reached the counter to ask for help, it was already too late for Boomer.

They were married on August 8 in the chapel of the Elks Street Baptist Church with their families and a few close friends in attendance. Two weeks later they loaded Elizabeth's few belongings into Boomer's car and drove to the apartment he had rented in Dallas. On the map the distance from Garland to Dallas is only twenty miles, but in terms of the new life they would find there, it might as well have been a million.

As Elizabeth spotted the sign for Grace Community Church, her thoughts returned to the present. She recognized most of the two dozen or so cars parked in the lot as belonging to various members of the women's Bible study group. She felt a little thrill of excitement as she anticipated sharing her dream and asking the women to join her in prayer for the young man whom she was so certain had been in an accident that morning.

When the study ended and Mary Beth Cummings asked if anyone had a prayer request, Elizabeth raised her hand. As she talked, Elizabeth examined the faces of the women who had been her friends and prayer partners for the past twelve years. She had expected them to show some interest as she retold her dream and asked them to pray with her for the young man, but as she searched those familiar faces, the only emotions that Elizabeth could detect were embarrassment and irritation.

When Elizabeth had finished talking, Mary Beth looked uncomfortable. "Well," she said tersely, "Why don't you lead us, Elizabeth, and we'll agree with you." As she prayed, Elizabeth knew that she was praying alone. No one was agreeing with her; they thought that she was behaving foolishly, and they wanted the prayer to end.

During dinner that evening Elizabeth told Boomer and the girls about her dream and having gotten out of bed to pray. She also told them about the cold reception she had received at the women's Bible study.

The girls looked at each other out of the corners of their eyes but remained silent. Boomer looked serious when he spoke, "Lizzie, I know that you mean well, and maybe someone did have an accident, but other people don't understand these things. When you talk like that, people think you're kind of crazy. If you want to pray for this person, go ahead, but don't talk about it to other people."

Elizabeth was quiet for the remainder of the meal. Afterwards, while the girls did the dishes, she went to the master bedroom on the third floor of their Charleston Single House and walked out onto the large balcony that extended across the front. The air was fragrant with roses and honeysuckle, and she sank down into one of the comfortable wicker chairs and breathed deeply. She thought about crying but realized that she did not really feel the need for tears. She felt dead inside. As she sat staring into the dark, she knew that no one was going to take her seriously.

Finally, she put her head back and closed her eyes, "Dear Jesus, I believe that I'm supposed to pray for this young man. Everyone thinks I'm crazy, but that's not important. I'm going to pray for him until I believe that you've shown me that I'm supposed to stop. From now on, it's just you and me together in this, but that's okay with me, because you're all I need."

Chapter 4

James was drifting in and out of awareness. It wasn't that he was losing consciousness; it was more like he was losing blocks of time. People kept asking him about his accident, but he was tired of repeating the story. Someone was telling him that they were going to have to cut off his clothes, and someone was washing him. A man's voice directed at someone else said that they had to pull the bone back inside his leg. "This is going to hurt," a voice cautioned him.

Pain like a thousand red-hot knives shot through his leg. James groaned through clenched teeth. "Wow! That's good," someone said, "usually people scream their heads off when we do that." James was confused, and for the first time he realized that everything looked dark and blurry and he couldn't focus his eyes.

"Are my mom and dad here?" he said to no one in particular.

"They're on their way," a woman's voice answered.

"Can I have something for the pain?"

"Sorry. You have to go into surgery. We can't give you anything right now."

Then he felt a presence close to his head and a woman's voice spoke. "I'm praying for you."

The voice sounded calm and sweet, but for the first time James felt scared. "It must be bad," he thought. "If they're like sending for a priest or something they must think I'm gonna die."

Ten minutes later James' parents were standing over him and his mother was gently stroking his face. "Are you in pain, Jimmy?" she asked.

"Yes, I need something, but they won't give me anything."

James's dad tried to sound authoritative as he spoke, "You're just fine. They have to do a little surgery to repair your leg, but you're just fine, son."

The nurse arrived to send the parents to the waiting room and someone wheeled James to the OR. Today everything was a big fuzzy blur. Tomorrow James would not remember most of it.

John Wesley and Barbara Goodwin were the only ones in the waiting room. Barbara was glad for that. She would have hated to try to pretend to be interested in someone else's family member when the only thing she cared about in the whole world at that moment was James. James, her second son—her baby.

Barbara's father-in-law was a Methodist preacher who came from a long line of Methodists. Like so many Methodist sons, he was named John Wesley after the founder of Methodism. Likewise, her husband had also been named

John Wesley. When their first son was born, her husband had insisted that he be John Wesley III. She knew that trying to convince him that there were already enough John Wesleys in the world would be a losing battle, so she gave in. Five years later she became pregnant with another son, and she was determined that he was going to be named after someone in her family. Her older brother James had died in a traffic accident when he was seventeen years old, and Barbara had grieved for him for a long time. She wanted to name this son James Arthur after him. Now as she sat waiting for her son to come out of surgery she wondered whether in naming him after her brother she had somehow jinxed him. Was he going to die too? Was the surgeon going to walk into the room with that grim expression that means, "He's dead"? The more she thought about it, the more frightened Barbara became.

Barbara was not much for prayer. She prayed at church and repeated The Lord's Prayer every morning before she began her day, but apart from that, she did not rely much on prayer. Barbara had a theory that God was going to do whatever He wanted to anyway, so it didn't matter much whether people prayed or not.

Now things looked different to her. "Oh God, don't let him die. Don't let him die. Don't let him die," she repeated over and over again. Tears were streaming down her face but she was not making any noise. She would have been embarrassed to sob or pray aloud. Her prayer was inside her head, and she hoped that it was somehow making its way to heaven.

It was both the longest and shortest six hours of Barbara's life. She felt that she had been sitting in that cold sterile waiting room for an eternity; yet, she had no idea how much time had passed. She had neither eaten nor drunk anything, but she felt neither hungry nor thirsty. She knew that she needed to call James' brother and sister, but she could not bear to talk to them until the surgery was over. She was barely holding herself together, and she could not give them a pep talk and try to convince them that everything was going to be fine.

When the surgeon finally came through the door, Barbara knew at once that James had made it through the surgery. Dr. Fleming looked tired, but he was not braced to deliver bad news. He assured Barbara and John Wesley that the surgery had gone well—better than expected. It would be a few days before they knew whether there had been any brain damage, but James was conscious and lucid before the surgery so that was a good sign.

"Did anyone tell you about his injuries?" Dr. Fleming asked.

"No," John Wesley answered, "the police told us that James had been in an accident, and we've been sitting here waiting for someone to come and talk to us."

The doctor began a description of James's injuries: His right femur was broken completely through in two places and had protruded through the skin under his hip. His right hip was broken and all of his ribs on his right side were cracked. The first surgery was to "clean him up." James was receiving antibiotics and the doctors were going to watch him for a few days to make certain that he did not have an infection in the bone. During that time his leg would remain in traction. After the surgical team had an opportunity to evaluate the x-rays and monitor James' progress, they would go in again and repair the damage.

"I've told the nurse to keep him heavily sedated for the next twenty-four hours," Dr. Fleming said. "He needs rest, and he's going to be in a lot of pain. You can see him, but he won't know you're here. You might want to go home and make some phone calls. Try to get some rest yourselves; you're probably going to be up here a lot for the next few days."

Chapter 5

On Monday morning after Boomer had left for work and Elizabeth had dropped the girls off at school, she returned home for her private prayer time. The cleaning lady came on Mondays so Elizabeth used that day to do pretty much as she pleased. When she entered the front door, she could hear the sound of dishes clattering in the kitchen and birds chirping through the open windows.

As glad as she was that Martina was taking care of the housework, Elizabeth wanted to be alone. Picking up her prayer list and a couple of notebooks, she headed down the flagstone path that led to the gazebo behind the house. Even though they had moved in more than ten years ago, Elizabeth had never grown accustomed to the beauty of the house and grounds. The large three-story structure built in the Charleston Single House style with its wide porches extending across the front on each level was welcoming and warm. Every time she came up the driveway, Elizabeth realized how blessed she had been. As impressive as the front of the house was, however, it was the gazebo near the back of the property that she especially loved. It was like having her own secret garden. The small white structure sitting on its slightly elevated bluestone base was the ultimate private escape. There among the flowering vines and enormous trees she could shut out the rest of the world and seek God.

As Elizabeth began to pray, her thoughts turned to the young man from her dream. "Well," she said aloud, "I can't continue to call him the young man from my dream. I'm going to have to give him a name." What should she call a young man whom she was not even sure existed? As she pondered this question, she suddenly thought about Timothy from the Bible. Paul called Timothy his "spiritual son." That was it! She would call the young man Timothy, and he would be her spiritual son.

Picking up one of the new notebooks, Elizabeth made an entry on the first page: "The Timothy Diary." Turning the page she wrote, "Friday, May 5, 2011. I woke up around 5:00 in the morning from a strange dream..." Elizabeth filled the following pages with a detailed account of the dream and the events that had followed at her prayer group and at dinner that evening with Boomer and the girls. She wrote about her conviction that the young man was real and about her decision to pray for him daily until God told her to stop. As she wrote, Elizabeth settled in her own heart the question of whether Timothy was "real." By the time she had finished pouring herself onto those pages, she was as sure of Timothy's existence as she was of her own girls'.

Finally, she was interrupted by the sound of Martina's footsteps on the flagstone path. For the first time she wondered why Martina chose to stand on her feet all day in hard-soled shoes. "At least," she thought, "she'll never be able to sneak up on me."

Martina was smiling, "I'm leaving now, Ms. Anderson, unless you need something?"

Elizabeth looked startled, "Is it that late already?"

"It's 4:30."

"Did you get your check? I left it on the kitchen counter."

"Yes, I did. Thank you."

"Okay. I'll see you next week."

Elizabeth followed Martina down the path to the house. As she entered the back door, she detected the faint aroma of lemon cleaner. It made the whole house smell fresh, and she almost hated to cover it up by cooking dinner.

While Elizabeth was making a salad, she realized that she had spent so much time on her diary entry for May 5 that she had forgotten to make an entry for Saturday, May 6. On that day she had felt that Timothy needed some special prayer and she had devoted almost an hour to praying for him before she felt that he was out of danger. She picked up her diary and made the entry. "I think," she said aloud, "that the only way to do this is to pray every day but make entries only for the days that I feel a special urgency to lift him up." That having been settled, she went back to washing lettuce.

Chapter 6

After three weeks and a second surgery James' parents took him to their home in Ft. Worth to continue his recovery. Barbara had made up his childhood room for him, and John Wesley had rented a wheelchair which he had positioned next to the bed. The room was exactly as he had left it three years earlier when he was seventeen—bunk beds, nondescript gray carpet, a worn wooden dresser pushed against the wall. Even the window was positioned oddly so that the only view was of a small patch of sky with a telephone wire running through the middle. It was a depressing room.

James couldn't believe that he was going to be stuck there for the next few months. His parents were good people, but they didn't understand him. His dad was lenient and had made few demands on his children, perhaps to compensate for the harsh treatment he had received from his own father. His mother was a moral woman, but she had never had a personal relationship with Christ. She and his dad attended the Methodist church regularly, but it was more out of habit than anything else. Like most of their friends, they believed that kids have to party and have some fun, but, in the end, they will turn out alright. They had expected little from their children and had gotten even less.

For as long as James could remember he had resented going to church. One Sunday afternoon when he was fourteen, he had complained bitterly about how much he hated church and all of the "hypocrites" who went there, and his parents had told him that he didn't have to attend any longer if he didn't want to. That was the last time he had set foot inside a church.

Suddenly, James imagined that his mother might try to force him to go to church with his dad and her on Sunday. He was much too sick to go anywhere, but he envisioned her coming into his room, dragging him into his wheelchair, pushing him down the aisle, and parking his chair next to their pew. The thought made his heart pound wildly. Even though James had long ago abandoned any notion that God had a personal interest in his life, there was a small gnawing feeling in the pit of his stomach that maybe God was keeping count. What if there were some huge cosmic computer that was recording everything that happened? What if God had let him live just so that He could torment him?

James' thoughts were interrupted by his mother entering the room. "What can I do for you, Jimmy?" she said.

"Mom, don't call me Jimmy."

Barbara was undaunted. "Do you remember when you were a little boy and I called you my Jiminy Cricket? You were the cutest little thing. You just loved Jiminy Cricket. Every Sunday evening you watched *The Wonderful World of Disney* on television. You would get so excited when Jiminy

Cricket came on, and when he sang that song about 'I'm no fool,' you sang right along with him...."

James winced, but he knew that there was no shutting her up. As his mother prattled on, his mind drifted back to the summer he had turned seventeen. He had felt that he had to get out of Ft. Worth and had persuaded his parents to allow him to spend the summer with his sister, Shirley, in California. She was three years older than he and had gone to Hollywood to break into the movies. Shirley had been in Los Angeles for three years, but the closest she had gotten to the big time was when she had served Katie Holmes a veggie burger on the patio of a trendy restaurant where she worked as a waitress while waiting for her big break.

Shirley had acquired some very "cool" friends in L A, and on James' first night there she and her boyfriend introduced him to pot. In the weeks that followed James progressed on to crack cocaine and lots of beer. They partied every night, and James spent every day on the beach surfing and sleeping on the sand. By the end of July James had made up his mind that he would not return to Ft. Worth for his senior year of high school.

When the weather turned cold, James and three of his surfing buddies decided to drive across the country in an old Ford van with ripped seats and a filthy mattress in the back. By the time they got to Albuquerque, however, they had nearly run out of money. They stopped at a convenience store to spend what was left of their cash on beer and cigarettes, and while James was using the restroom, his buddies drove away and left him stranded.

That was how James got into the construction business. While he was standing in the parking lot wondering what to do next, a rough looking guy with a shaved head and arms covered in tattoos came out of the store. He opened the door of a truck with a sign on the side that read, "Castro Construction." James did not hesitate. He called out, "Hey, man. Do you know where I can get some work?"

The shaved head turned in his direction, and James found himself looking into the coldest pair of eyes he had ever seen. "You know how to paint?"

"Sure," James replied with a great deal more confidence than he felt. The truth was that he had never painted anything in his life, but how hard could it be? You dip the brush in the paint and wipe it on the wall, right?

"Get in," the shaved head ordered.

James obeyed, but he immediately felt that he had made a mistake. The shaved head neither looked at him nor spoke, and James imagined that he was taking him to some remote place to rob and murder him. As scared as he was, he thought, "If he's planning to rob me, the joke's on him."

James was on the verge of complete panic when they arrived at a construction site, and the shaved head stopped the truck. Four guys were working on a house that was nearing completion, and they eyed James with little interest as he followed the shaved head up the walk to the front door. The shaved head spoke to a small muscular worker in his mid-thirties, "Munoz, this dude says he can paint. Put him to work."

Munoz's dark eyes surveyed James skeptically, "Sure, boss."

Without another word the shaved head walked back to the truck and drove away.

James felt a little safer with the shaved head gone, and he smiled at Munoz as he shifted his weight from foot to foot. "I'm James. Here to paint. Ready to goooo!"

Munoz just stared at him. "Get this room primed. Everything's over there in the corner."

The room was large with high ceilings and a massive fireplace. It was an expensive house—the nicest one James had ever been in. He needed this job and didn't want to mess up; he had a feeling that if he did, the shaved head was not going to take it well. The problem was that James had no idea what Munoz was talking about. How do you prime a room?

When he was a little boy and had visited his grandparents' farm, he had helped his grandfather prime the pump by pouring water over it. He also knew that prime meat was "really good", but none of this information gave him a clue as to how to prime a room.

Finally, he approached Munoz. "Sorry, man, but uh, like, what am I supposed to do?"

Munoz remained silent for a few moments and then called to one of the other workers, "Grady, get him started."

Grady was about James' age with long dirty hair and an even dirtier tee shirt covered with obscenities. He smiled. It was the first smile James had seen since he discovered that his friends had left him at the convenience store. Grady had been on the crew for six months, and his only interest was in making enough money to get high. He had been looking for someone to split the cost of a cheap motel room so that he could crash indoors; the minute he laid eyes on James, he knew that he was the answer to his problem.

That night after work James and Grady smoked pot together and slept on the street. Grady shared his plan with James for pooling their money when they got paid on Friday and renting a room at the Albuquerque Inn. The following eight months were spent working for the shaved head during the day and getting high at night in the privacy of the crumbling walls of the Albuquerque Inn.

Chapter 7

James' mother entered his room carrying a tray with soup, crackers, and iced tea. "I want you to eat this, Jimmy," she announced. "You need to get your strength back."

James nodded and tried to look convincing, but he was so sick that he knew he would not be able to eat anything. He was nauseated, and the pain in his leg and ribs was blinding.

"Mom, I need something for the pain."

"I have your prescription that Dr. Fleming gave you when we left the hospital, but you can't have any more until 8:00."

"That's two hours away, Mom. I can't wait two hours."

"I'll call the doctor in the morning and see if we can get you something stronger."

"I'll be dead by morning."

"No, you won't! Stop talking like that, Jimmy. The doctor said that you are going to have to learn to deal with the pain until you get better. Eventually, it will go away, but until then you are going to have to live with it."

"I can't! You've never been in pain like this. You don't know what I'm going through. I wish I was dead!"

"Don't say that, Jimmy. You're lucky to be alive, and you're going to get well. It's just going to take some time. I'll bring you your pills at eight." With that Barbara walked out of the room and shut the door.

As James lay in his bed with the pillows propped under his leg to try to give him some relief, he thought about the morning of the accident. The really ironic part was that it was probably the only time in the last year that he had ridden his bike when he wasn't high. He did not want his parents to know that he was into drugs, and he had not used during his three-day visit. When he had left that morning, he was planning to ride out of town and pull over at the first rest stop to get high.

After his second surgery the doctor ordered a morphine drip that kept him pain free, warm, and blissful, but after a few days, a nurse came and took it away. That's when the pain became intolerable. He begged for something to help him, but the pills that the nurse dispensed in the little white paper cup might as well have been baby aspirin.

Those pills were now his sole pain medication. James covered his face with his hands and said, "Oh, my God! What am I going to do?" James wasn't really speaking to God; he wasn't praying or asking for direction, but he was feeling such despair that the words simply slipped out. Fortunately for him, although he would not see any changes for a long time, God was listening.

Chapter 8

The doctor refused to prescribe stronger pain medication and told Barbara that when James finished his prescription he would not renew it. James was going to have to learn to "deal with his discomfort."

When Barbara gave James the news, he began crying— not the tears of a grown man who was overcome by grief or disappointment. The room was filled with the loud wet sobs of an out-of-control child.

Barbara was alarmed by James' reaction, and she sat on his bed and cradled his head in her arms. "It's alright, Jimmy. Mama's here."

"Please help me! I can't live like this. Please, Mom. I mean it! I can't live like this! Will you help me?"

"What do you want me to do?"

In that moment James knew that he had won a victory. "I want you to get me some pot. In New Mexico medical marijuana is legal. Everybody uses it to help them with pain and nausea. If I had some pot, I could get through this."

"Jimmy!" his mother replied. "It's not legal here. I'm not going to get marijuana for you. You know how your father and I feel about that kind of thing."

"The only reason it's not legal here is because Texas is full of Baptists and Nazis that are against everything! I hate Texas! They want to control everybody!"

James became so distraught that Barbara finally agreed to talk to his father.

That evening she told John Wesley that the doctor had refused to increase the pain medication. She then described James' outburst and said that she didn't know what to do.

To her surprise, John Wesley said, "I don't know why it's such a big deal. James is right. A lot of states allow medical marijuana now. It's probably a lot safer than most of the stuff you see advertised on TV. The side effects of nearly everything they sell are worse than what they're trying to cure."

"You think we should let him have it?"

"Why not?"

"Let me talk to him first," Barbara replied.

She rose from her chair and walked into James' room. "Daddy thinks it would be okay for us to get you some marijuana to help you through this, but before we do, I want you to make me a promise.

James was stunned. He could not believe that it had been that easy. "Okay."

"Jimmy, I want you to promise me that just as soon as you get through this bad period you will stop using marijuana and that you will never use any other drugs ever again."

James eyed her suspiciously, "Sure."

"No, Jimmy. I want you to promise me."

"Okay."

"Say it. Say, 'I promise.'"

"I promise."

For the first time Barbara smiled, "I'll tell Daddy. You know I love you, Jimmy, and I don't want you to suffer, but if I thought that I did something that turned you into a junkie, I would never forgive myself."

"Don't worry, Mom. That won't happen."

Barbara told her husband that she had made James promise her that as soon as he was better he would stop using marijuana and that he would never use any other drugs.

"Did you believe him?"

"Of course, I believe him. Jimmy has never lied to me."

"Are you sure of that?"

"Yes!" Barbara was becoming agitated so John Wesley dropped it.

Later than evening he went into James' room to talk about getting him the marijuana. John Wesley was a high school algebra teacher, and he was well aware that most of his students smoked pot. He knew the chances were nearly one-hundred percent that his kids used drugs to some extent. He had never said anything to Barbara because he knew that she would panic, but he had seen enough of how kids live to not cling to any illusions about his own children's lifestyles.

The real purpose of his talk with James was to find out how he could get the pot with the least amount of risk. John Wesley was fifty years old—only five years away from retirement, and he could not afford to get arrested and lose his job with the Ft. Worth Independent School District.

James chose his words carefully. "I've got this friend Grady that I work with. He knows a pharmacist, and he can get it for me. I'm supposed to have a prescription, but they're real close, and I think he'll do it for me. It'll cost more though."

James had looked down the whole time he was talking so that he could not see the expression on John Wesley's face. "Save that crap for your mother!" John Wesley snapped. "The only reason we're having this conversation is so that I can get your pot without ending up in jail."

James continued to look down. "I'll call Grady. He'll get it down here. He knows which checkpoints in New Mexico aren't manned. I'll let you know how much it'll cost."

John Wesley turned and walked out of the room. James' visit had been uncomfortable, and John Wesley had been relieved that morning when he had climbed onto his motorcycle to return to Angel Fire. The accident had been stressful beyond belief, and now James was making things worse by demanding that he supply him with illegal drugs. John Wesley couldn't wait for his son to go back to Angel Fire.

Chapter 9

*L*ate in the afternoon of January 9 James piled his clothes into the backseat of the ten-year-old Ford that John Wesley had bought for him and began the trip to Angel Fire. His doctor had released him the week before, and he was anxious to get out of Ft. Worth. He would have left that same day if he had been able to procure a vehicle, but he had been at the mercy of his parents to provide him with transportation.

John Wesley had been resigned to doing whatever was necessary to get James out of the house—even if it meant spending twenty-five hundred dollars for the abused red Focus with the peeling paint and threadbare seats. He was concerned only with getting James away from him; if he broke down as soon as he crossed the New Mexico State line, that was James' problem. He could call Grady for help from now on.

Barbara was a bundle of emotions as James pulled out of the driveway. Tears streamed down her cheeks as she smiled and told him that she loved him. She did love him, but James had been an unwelcome disruption to her life. She had been his nursemaid and had spent the last eight months fetching and carrying for him. She had washed his clothes and cooked his meals, and tried to keep peace between him and John Wesley. Besides, James looked like what he was—a shiftless little druggie—and Barbara was embarrassed by him. She had always told her friends that her children were doing "very well", but anyone who saw James knew instantly that he was devoid of both prospects and ambition. Although a part of her was genuinely sad to see him go, a much bigger part was relieved to have her life back.

James was not exactly happy to be headed back to Angel Fire. He had not experienced anything that resembled happiness for years. He was angry, not because he had anything to be angry about, but because he had formed a habit of being angry. For the past three years he had been angry when he awakened every morning and angry when he went to sleep every night. He was cynical and negative and miserable in a way that had become so much a part of him that it felt normal. Allowing all that anger and resentment to wash over him as he drove north on Highway 35 gave him an odd feeling of contentment.

According to a website that his mom had consulted, the driving distance between Ft. Worth and Angel Fire is 516.6 miles. "That's the dumbest thing I ever heard of!" James thought. "Who comes up with those extra six tenths of a mile? What if I live on the far side of Ft. Worth? This is why I can't stand people. They're all idiots. They control the Zombies like my mom and dad who actually believe that it is 516.6 miles."

Normally, James would have driven straight through, but he was not fully recovered, and after downing a Big Mac and super-sized fries in Amarillo, he pulled into a rest stop to smoke a joint and fell asleep. It was after 6:00 A.M. before he was on the road again. The roads north of Albuquerque were icy, and James' tires were old, so it was slow going on the last leg of the trip.

It was after 3:00 P.M. when James emerged from Carson National Forest and began the slight descent into Angel Fire. The sun was sparkling on random patches of snow, and a brisk wind drove the cold air through the inch space where the passenger window refused to close. James was more than ready for his trip to end. As he rounded the curve that would give him a clear view of the dilapidated house that he shared with Grady and whoever else was around to help pay the rent, James felt a slight thrill of expectation. That sensation quickly evaporated, however, when he spotted several police cars and Grady standing in the front yard in handcuffs. James looked straight ahead and kept driving.

"Grady! You idiot!" James muttered under his breath.

Every time that Grady had brought pot to James while he was in Ft. Worth, James had quoted John Wesley a much higher price than the current street value. He had collected the cash from his dad, given half to Grady and pocketed the rest. He had told Grady that he was giving him everything and that he was to save half for him so that he would have some cash when he got back to Angel Fire. It was a good deal for James since he and Grady were growing the pot in the basement of their rental house and supporting themselves by dealing.

As he headed back toward Taos, James vowed that he would never see that loser Grady again. He had enough cash to last him for a while and a big world to explore. "Maybe I'll find me a nice warm beach," he thought. For the first time in weeks, he smiled.

Chapter 10

On May 23 Molly Anderson celebrated her eighteenth birthday, and a week later she graduated from Harlan Stringer High School. Until Molly's junior year, Elizabeth had looked forward to her graduation. She and Boomer had always assumed that their girls would live at home while they earned their degrees from Baylor, and she had thought their college years would be a wonderful part of their lives together as a family. They had talked about Baylor since Molly was a little girl, and there had never been any doubt that this was where they expected her to go.

During her junior year in high school, however, Molly had told her parents that she wanted to earn a degree in interior design and then join Boomer in his firm. On the surface, it sounded like a good plan, but Elizabeth had the uneasy feeling that Molly was playing them. Although she did not say so, Elizabeth suspected that Molly's only real interest was in getting out from under her parents' control.

Six years earlier Boomer had left Dungee, Harris, and Schmidt to open his own firm. He had earned an excellent reputation for his creative designs, and Bradley Anderson and Associates had been successful from the start. The last time anyone had called Boomer "Bradley" was at his christening, but he had thought that "Boomer Anderson and Associates" sounded a little too folksy. He had compromised by having his name on his business cards read "Bradley (Boomer) Anderson".

When he and Elizabeth had first married, Boomer had imagined that he would have a son to take into the architectural firm that he hoped to eventually open. Although he loved his girls very much, he had always been a little disappointed that he was never going to realize that dream. Molly knew this and took full advantage of her father's desire to have Bradley Anderson and Associates stay in the family. When Molly had said that she wanted to join the firm as an interior designer, he was thrilled and immediately began telling both friends and business associates that as soon as Molly had her degree she was going to join the firm. "There won't be an architectural firm in California that will be able to offer its clients more," he boasted.

Elizabeth did not want to tell Boomer that she thought Molly was lying about her motives for going to design school. She believed that her interest in the Academy of Art University in San Francisco had less to do with her desire to earn a degree in interior design than it did with the fact that her boyfriend Dustin was going to Stanford in the fall. With Stanford less than forty miles away, they would have ample opportunities to spend time together.

Every time Elizabeth tried to persuade Molly to change her mind about not going to Baylor, her daughter recited a long list of objections. This made Elizabeth even more suspicious. When Molly began saying that she would not go to Baylor because the kids who went there were "too corrupt," Elizabeth knew that her objections were a smoke screen to hide her real motives. According to Molly, she could not bear to go to a school that had a reputation as a Christian University but where the students and faculty were "hypocrites".

If Molly had only said that she wanted to go to school in San Francisco to be near Dustin, Elizabeth would have been much less worried. She would not have agreed to allow her to go, but she would have been less worried. "At least," she thought, "that would have been honest." More than anything, it was Molly's lying that worried her. The truth was that Elizabeth believed that Molly had been lying to her for a long time. She had been dating Dustin for eighteen months, and Elizabeth was certain that they were having sex. She had asked Molly about it on several occasions, but her daughter had always reacted with a great show of indignation and denied any wrongdoing.

Elizabeth and Boomer had taught the girls that sex outside of marriage is always wrong, and they had let them know that they expected them to remain celibate until marriage. They had talked about how God's laws concerning extra-marital sex protect society on many levels. They had discussed the moral issues, the health issues, and the social issues. At every opportunity Elizabeth had emphasized these points to her daughters. She had not "beaten them over the head," but whenever the subject came up, she used the opportunity to reinforce those lessons.

Molly had always been difficult. She had been a beautiful baby and had remained beautiful through every stage of her life. Her long blonde hair and eyes the color of Windex made her a real head-turner. Just about everyone who saw her agreed that she was beautiful. Women complimented Elizabeth on Molly's beauty, and men stood staring at her as if they were hypnotized. Wherever she went, she received an inordinate amount of attention. Yet, for Molly it was not enough to be a beautiful young woman; she wanted to be the only beautiful young woman.

Molly's younger sister Tracy was easily as beautiful as she, but Molly spent much of her time trying to make Tracy feel bad about herself. When Tracy was twelve, Molly had told her that she looked like a homeless person. Tracy had cried, and Elizabeth had comforted her—assuring her that no one would ever mistake her for a bag lady.

It wasn't that Molly did not have good qualities. She was unusually intelligent and witty, and she possessed an uncanny ability to impersonate almost anyone with an amazing degree of accuracy. Molly could twist her beautiful face into a variety of expressions so that she was able to make herself look old, stupid, and even fat whenever she wished. She could make the family laugh until tears ran down their faces, and at these times, she was in her element. Encouraged by their response, she would spend an entire evening performing for her audience of three.

Molly could be lots of fun, but she was also manipulative. She considered herself to be a master of manipulation; in fact, she was a mediocre manipulator at best. Her attempts were apparent to almost everyone, and to Elizabeth she was as transparent as glass. Boomer was the one person who always seemed to be taken in by her. She was, after all, his beautiful little girl, and he could not accept that she might be using him. Boomer preferred to take everything that Molly said at face value, and he was determined to support her decision to go to San Francisco to earn her degree.

Elizabeth was outnumbered. She knew that allowing Molly to follow Dustin to California was a bad idea, but she was unable to prevent her from going. In late August she kissed her oldest daughter good-by and put her on a plane for San Francisco.

Chapter 11

lizabeth was amazed to discover how peaceful the house had become since Molly had left. Tracy had begun her junior year, and Elizabeth feared that she would see the same behavior surface in Tracy that had dominated Molly's final high school years.

Tracy, however, was very different from her sister. She was as obedient as Molly was rebellious, and, although she was tempted at times to make bad choices, she never seriously considered abandoning her parents' teachings. Years later Elizabeth would say that while she had spent thousands of hours crying over Molly, Tracy had never caused her to shed a single tear.

As Thanksgiving approached, Molly told her parents that she could not come home for the holiday. She was working on a design project that would count for one-third of her grade, and she needed to devote the long weekend to finishing it. During her telephone conversation, she even gave them a detailed description of exactly what the project entailed. When Elizabeth asked her to e-mail a photo, however, Molly changed the subject.

Boomer accepted Molly's explanation without question, but Elizabeth felt more uneasy than ever. She knew that Molly was not going to be honest with them, so she pushed her suspicions out of her mind and began making plans for the holiday without her. Both sets of in-laws were invited and several elderly widows from the church accepted invitations to join them for Thanksgiving dinner.

That evening, after their guests were gone and Tracy had left with her friends to see the new Iron Man movie, Elizabeth and Boomer went for a long walk through the neighborhood. The air was cold and invigorating, and as she walked alongside Boomer with her small hand in his big warm one, Elizabeth was very content. She missed Molly, but her oldest daughter had become such a source of stress in the family that a small part of her was glad that she did not have to spend her holiday acting as a buffer between Molly and the other family members.

Thanksgiving came late that year, and the following week Elizabeth began preparing for Christmas. Although she was busy with the shopping, decorating, and meal planning, she could not shake the feeling that trouble was coming.

While she was working in the house or running errands, Elizabeth prayed. Because she was alone most of the time, she prayed aloud, entreating God to keep Molly safe and to help her make good choices. She believed that Molly was in trouble, but she had no proof. Boomer brushed aside her concerns, saying that she was just nervous because Molly was away from home for the first time, but Elizabeth knew that was not true. She had a cold feeling in the middle of her chest that she knew from experience signaled trouble.

Molly did not come home when the Christmas break began. She made an excuse about having to do some work to prepare for the spring semester. When she finally arrived on December 23, Elizabeth was alarmed to see how thin she had become, and she wondered whether she was anorexic. She knew that there was no point in asking her, so she decided to just watch her carefully and try to act as if everything were normal.

That evening after dinner as they sat in the large family room with the fire blazing in the fireplace and Christmas carols playing softly, Molly seemed more like her old self. She was talkative and smiling as she recounted stories of her classmates and professors. For the first time since Molly had left home, Elizabeth felt better. Maybe Boomer was right; maybe she was overreacting; maybe Molly was serious about earning her degree and working with Boomer; maybe she was not giving her daughter enough credit.

As Molly warmed to her audience, she kicked off her shoes and pulled her feet up on the maze-colored chenille sofa. When she did, her pant leg rode up a couple of inches, and Elizabeth caught sight of a butterfly tattoo on her ankle. Molly did not realize that her mother had seen her body art, and she quickly pulled down the hem of her pant leg and continued her patter. Instantly, Elizabeth felt the sense of dread descend on her once again.

The following days were typical of Christmas in the Anderson house. Immediately following the church service on Christmas Eve, Elizabeth, Boomer and the girls made the annual trek to view the Christmas lights. As usual, they finished their evening by sitting around the kitchen table sipping mugs of hot chocolate and nibbling assorted candies and cookies. On Christmas Day both sets of grandparents came for dinner. Gifts were exchanged, and everyone was in high spirits. Tracy and Molly helped Elizabeth in the kitchen, and there were moments when everything seemed normal.

If it had not been for that fleeting glimpse of the butterfly tattoo, Elizabeth might have been lulled into believing that she was wrong to worry about Molly. She would have had a difficult time explaining to someone else why she was so alarmed by that small patch of colored ink. It wasn't the tattoo that bothered Elizabeth—it was what the tattoo represented; Molly was casting aside everything that she and Boomer had spent a lifetime teaching her. Many teens had tattoos, and many of their parents did not object. For them having an ankle tattoo was simply a fashion statement. But Molly knew that her parents strongly objected to tattoos; for her to get a tattoo was a deliberate act of rebellion.

Elizabeth and Boomer had expected Molly to stay with them at least through New Year's Day, but the day after Christmas she announced that she had to be back at school by December 30.

"Why?" Elizabeth asked.

"I just do. I've got a lot of stuff to do to get ready for the new semester."

"What stuff? School doesn't start for another three weeks."

"I need to get started studying."

"You can't possibly start studying. You don't have any assignments. You don't even have your books yet. I want you to spend some time with us."

"I can't. I'm working to have a career, and I'm not going to let you stop me!" Molly's voice had grown shrill.

Elizabeth was certain that Molly's wanting to return to California had nothing to do with studying, but she did not pursue the subject further. Why was she being so secretive?

Molly was wound up tight, and she began a tirade. "I don't want to be here for New Years because I know you and Dad will be drunk and Tracy will be hanging out with her nerdy friends at the church party."

Elizabeth was shocked and angry. "What is the matter with you!" she shouted. "I have never been drunk in my life! You know that Dad and I don't drink anything with alcohol in it! How dare you! You're talking like a crazy person!"

At that moment Boomer walked through the front door, and both Molly and Elizabeth stopped talking.

Molly ran to Boomer and threw her arms around him. "Daddy! I need to talk to you."

"Okay, Sweetheart," Boomer replied.

"Alone, in your office," Molly responded.

The two of them walked down the hall, and Elizabeth heard their footsteps on the stairs. After a few moments, she heard the door to Boomer's study close.

On December 29 Molly boarded a plane for San Francisco. She had convinced Boomer to allow her to move to an apartment off campus by telling him that the dorm was so noisy that she could hardly study. There was a girl she had met at school who was looking for a roommate, and the apartment would be "just perfect".

Elizabeth was convinced that Molly would have moved off campus without telling them if they had not been paying all of her bills. As it was, Boomer would have to stop paying for the dorm and start sending a hefty stipend directly to Molly to cover her half of the rent on the pricey loft apartment. Elizabeth did not know it, but on the day that she left Boomer had given Molly a check for five thousand dollars for "moving expenses, and stuff."

Chapter 12

When James left Angel Fire, he drove south towards Albuquerque. Before he reached the city limits, he had decided that he would go to Florida. He had never been to Florida, but the idea of lounging on a Miami beach appealed to him. At Albuquerque he headed straight down I-25 to Las Cruces where he took Interstate 10 to El Paso. I-10 would take him all the way to Florida; if the map he had consulted were accurate, it would take him directly to the ocean. As James thought more about it, he decided that he might not go to Miami at all. I-10 would take him to Jacksonville where he could drive directly into the Atlantic Ocean. That would be the coolest thing ever: To drive all the way from El Paso to Jacksonville without ever making a turn and then to keep on driving—right into the ocean!

As James entered the El Paso city limits, he began thinking about lyrics to a song that would describe his journey. "I'm just cruise'n in my ride, with my posse by my side." Well, he didn't have anyone by his side—not even that dumb loser Grady, but that was hardly the point. This song would be his legacy, and he wanted to get it right. It would embody the contempt that he felt for society with all its rules and restrictions. It would make him into a folk hero. He would not pretend to die for any "cause." He would let the world know that he had preferred a watery death to an existence where he was bound by mindless regulations.

It was late and James was tired. He spotted a cheap motel off the interstate and took the exit. After picking up a pizza and checking into his room, he began writing the lyrics to his song on the pizza box. The next hours were spent writing lyrics and drinking beer.

James had no idea when he had fallen asleep. Daylight was streaming in through the window when he awoke still fully dressed lying across the bed with the half-eaten pizza and the remaining two cans of the six pack on the bedside table. After "breakfast" James climbed back into his car and continued east on I-10.

A funny thing happened on the way to James' suicide. When he got to San Antonio, he spotted flashing lights from a police car behind him. Within minutes the officer had cuffed him, put him in the back of his cruiser, and driven him to the station where he booked him on a DUI. James was terrified. He had never been arrested, and visions of being forced to be the "girlfriend" of a huge jailhouse bully named Bubba flashed before his eyes.

"Oh my God! What am I going to do?" James said as he sat with his eyes closed and his head in his hands. It was the second time in less than a year that James had asked that question.

James spent an uneventful night in the San Antonio jail surrounded by young guys very much like him. He was, however, certain that if he were sentenced to do jail time he would end up at the mercy of an enormous tyrant who ran the joint "like it was his own personal plaything". Consequently, when he appeared before the judge the following morning, he pulled out everything his parents had taught him about showing respect and good manners.

When Judge Robert Chavez asked him if he had anything to say, James replied, "Yes, your Honor. I was in a bad accident last May and almost died. At that time I started using medical marijuana to help me with the pain and nausea. I'm afraid that I kind of got to depend on it. I still have days with lots of pain, and I just haven't been able to get off pot because it's the only thing that helps. So I was wondering if maybe you could send me to rehab. If I could just get some help, I'm sure that I could get clean."

Judge Chavez stared thoughtfully at James before he answered. "I'm going to check out your story, and if you're telling me the truth about your accident, I'll send you to rehab."

James was taken to a room where he gave an officer of the court the details of his accident including the date, the location, and the name of the hospital and the doctor who had treated him. Then he was escorted back to his cell.

The next day James was moved to a rehab center where the court ordered him to remain until he was pronounced ready to be released. He was then to be taken back to court to appear before Judge Chavez. James was so relieved that he cried all the way to the rehab facility.

Rehab was not nearly as bad as James had imagined. He immediately made friends with a guy named Hunter who had some outside connections. Hunter was able to get some drugs smuggled in and, to James' delight, Hunter was willing to share.

One day while Hunter was in a counseling session James found a new Gideon Bible in the lounge. He picked it up and let if fall open at random. The page in front of him was the book of John, chapter 14 where Jesus said, "If you love Me, keep My commandments. And I will pray the Father, and He will give you another Comforter, that He may abide with you forever—the Spirit of truth, whom the world cannot receive."

As he read those words, James felt something stir inside him. It was as if a memory from his childhood, or, perhaps, from someone else's childhood, wanted to surface. He felt it as if it were a tangible thing stirring in his mind and his chest and his stomach. He wanted to cry. Instead, he closed the Bible and returned it to the table where he had found it.

The following day James returned to the lounge, and as soon as he walked through the door, he spotted the Bible still lying on the table. James quickly picked it up and, again, allowed it to fall open. Before him was John 14, "If you love Me, keep my Commandments. And I will pray the Father, and He will give you another Comforter, that He may abide with you forever—the Spirit of truth, whom the world cannot receive."

Again and again James allowed the Bible to fall open, and every time it fell open to that same spot. "If you love Me....I will pray the Father....give you another Comforter...the Spirit of truth." James' hands were shaking.

Keeping his voice as steady as possible, he turned to another inmate and said, "Hey, man, let this fall open and see what happens." The Bible fell open to chapter 3 of Isaiah.

"Do it again." This time it fell open to Matthew, chapter 1.

"One more time, Man." It fell open to I Samuel, chapter 2.

"Thanks." James took the Bible back and sat down with it on his lap. He felt a little less nervous as he allowed it to fall open once again. When he saw that the page before him was John 14, he felt his hair stand on end.

James did not know what he should do next. He had given up both God and religion a long time ago, but if anyone ever needed comforting, it was he. He quickly walked back to his room, leaving the Bible on the table.

Chapter 13

James ran his right hand nervously through his thick, wavy, golden-brown hair. For the first time in years his hair was short and clean. He sat on the bench outside Judge Chavez's chambers chewing the already gnawed fingernails on his left hand as his right hand continued to run through his hair. His heart was pounding, and he felt as if he were going to be sick. He had managed to complete his rehab, and the center had released him to the court. It was now up to Judge Chavez to decide his fate.

"I'll probably have a heart attack and die right here," James thought as he sat beside the officer who had transported him from the rehab center to the courthouse. James was trying to control his breathing, but without much success. "I'll be just another guy from rehab who died waiting for some crazy old judge to ruin his life. They probably won't even put my name in the paper. Mom and Dad will never know what happened to me. I'll never be able to drive off I-10 into the Atlantic. It was my one dream, and now Texas has taken that away from me!"

By the time he was ushered into Judge Chavez' chambers, James was on the verge of tears. Fortunately, the judge interpreted James' demeanor to be a sign of remorse for his past actions, and he was, consequently, inclined to show him leniency.

After a ten-minute discussion, Judge Chavez ordered James to serve one year probation. "Stay out of trouble," he cautioned, "report to your probation officer, and a year from now you'll be free. But I want you to understand one thing, young man; I do not, I repeat, do not, want to see you in here again. Do you understand?"

"Yes, your Honor. Thank you."

"Don't thank me; thank God. He's the one who saved your neck."

When the judge spoke those words, James felt something like a little jolt of electricity pass through his body. He wished that the judge had said almost anything but that. He could have berated James for being a scummy little punk; he could have called him a filthy little druggie, he could have said almost anything and it would not have upset James as much as that simple statement.

James looked down. "Yes, your Honor."

The judge handed James a piece of paper with a name and a phone number on it. "When you appeared in my court on January 12, you gave your profession as 'house painter'. This is the name and phone number of one of the best builders in San Antonio. I've already talked to him, and he said that he would give you a chance. Remember, James, keeping a job is a condition of your probation. Don't let me down."

"Yes, your Honor."

As James left Judge Chavez' chambers, he was more frightened than he had ever been in his life. Maybe he would have been better off taking his chances in jail.

Chapter 14

$\mathcal{B}$illy Ferguson was a big man with a barrel chest and a booming voice. His small blue eyes and square head with its rim of white hair gave him a fierce appearance, and if it had not been for the nearly perpetual smile that spread across his broad face, he would have been intimidating.

James sat across the gray metal desk from Billy answering his questions. As the interview progressed, James had the uncomfortable feeling that Billy was more interested in his personal life than he was in his painting skills. He asked numerous questions about his family, his friends, and his accident. This was not a job interview; it was an interrogation.

James' eyes darted about the small office located in Billy's trailer on the job site. Nearly every inch of the wall space was taken up by a plaque or a bumper sticker: "Smile, God Loves You." "This is the Day that the Lord has Made; We will Rejoice and be Glad in It." "Christians aren't perfect; they're Just Forgiven." "Jesus is Lord." "Real Men Pray."

After what seemed like an eternity, Billy concluded the interview and took James outside to introduce him to a young man of about twenty who looked like a younger version of Billy.

"James here is going to be painting for us," Billy announced. "Show him around and get him started."

Turning to James, Billy said, "You have any questions, you ask Tracer. He's the best there is."

After Billy had returned to his office and closed the door, James looked at Tracer more closely. "You known Billy long?" James asked.

"All my life. He's my granddad."

"How is it? Working for your granddad, I mean?"

"It's good. I'm lucky to be here. My granddad raised me, and whenever I wasn't in school I was on the job site with him. I've been around construction since I was six."

"Why?"

"Well, when you have to go to work with your granddad, and your granddad is a builder, you end up spending most of your life on a construction site."

"No, I mean why did your granddad raise you?"

"My dad left before I was born, and my mom died when I was five. My grandma got killed in a car wreck a few months later. That just left me and granddad."

"Do you ever see your dad?"

"When he took off, that was it. I've never even met him. The only thing I have of his is his last name. Mack. My name's Tracer Mack. Odd name isn't it?"

"I guess. I've heard worse."

As James and Tracer talked, they had been walking toward what was going to be the new location of Riley's Steak House. It was modern and trendy, yet with a rustic vibe that was distinctly Texas. When they entered, James felt a sense of peace and calm that he had not known for a long time.

"Where're you staying?" Tracer asked.

"I dunno; I'll find something."

"You're on probation. You have to have a real address to give to your probation officer. They're not going to play games with you."

"I've got some money. I'll find a place."

"My granddad owns some apartments a couple of miles from here. They're not fancy, but they're clean and fully furnished, and the rent's cheap. We have one that's vacant. Are you interested?"

"Sure."

"I'll take you by after work."

James spent the afternoon prepping the walls of the main dining room. The following morning he would begin painting. He noticed the name of the color on the cans stacked against the back wall—serenity. "What's the color of serenity?" James wondered.

At 6:00 Tracer entered the room where James was working and informed him that it was time to go. James quickly cleaned up his area and stacked his work materials neatly in the corner. "What color's serenity?" he asked.

"Huh?"

"The paint. The cans say 'serenity'."

"It's kind of gray."

"Why are we painting the dining room gray?"

"Serenity is my granddad's favorite paint color because he says it goes with everything. We're using a lot of dark wood and stainless steel in this area. The paint will complement both the wood and the steel. It will add a little bit of color because it's got a slight purple undertone, but when it's on the wall, most people think it's gray."

Tracer took James to his truck—an old model Ford. When James climbed into the cab on the passenger side, he was surprised to see that Tracer shared his granddad's love of Christian bumper stickers. The dashboard was covered with them: "Turn or Burn." "Life is Fragile; Handle with Prayer." "Honk if you Love Jesus."

"Why do you have a bumper sticker on your dash that says, 'Honk if You Love Jesus?' Nobody can see it, and nobody's ever gonna honk."

"You can see it. Be my guest, and honk when you're ready." Tracer motioned toward the steering wheel, but James turned and stared out the passenger window. In the future, he would need to be more careful about what he said to Tracer.

James did not speak again until they arrived at the apartments. When Tracer pulled the truck around to a building at the back of the complex, James was surprised to see that one of the tenants had a beat-up red Ford Focus exactly like his; then he blinked and stared at the peeling paint and dented left rear fender. All sorts of thoughts raced through James' mind: Someone had stolen his car from the police impound lot, and the thief was living in these apartments!

"That's my car!" he shouted.

"I know. Granddad got it out for you. He said that you were going to need it, and there was no sense in your keeping on running up charges until payday. He'll take a little out of your check each week until you get him paid back. He's got the receipt for you showing how much he paid to get it out."

"How could he do that? It's my property. Why would they turn it over to him?"

"Judge Chavez sent down an order to have it released to Granddad."

"They must be pretty thick," James said suspiciously.

"They're about as thick as people get," Tracer responded.

"Yeah, why's that?"

"Well, Granddad married Judge Chavez's sister, who was my grandma, when the judge was about sixteen. My granddad was kind of like the big brother the judge never had."

James felt as if he were trapped in a nightmare from which he could not escape. He wished he could wake up and discover that the last few weeks had never happened. He wanted to open his eyes and find himself lying fully clothed across the bed in the flea-bag motel in El Paso where he had begun writing his song. He promised himself that if by some miracle he did manage to wake up, he would never attempt to go to Florida.

Chapter 15

When Molly returned to San Francisco, she called to say that she had gotten back safely. Boomer had answered the phone, and she had assured him that she loved him and that he was "the best Daddy in the whole world."

After that it became increasingly difficult for her parents to contact her. She rarely answered her cell phone, so the preferred method of communication became e-mails. On the rare occasions when she did pick up the phone, she was friendly and chatty, but she revealed almost nothing about her life. She talked about how busy she was and discussed design projects that she was working on for school, but she never mentioned her roommate or professors. She would occasionally reference, "a friend of mine" but never gave a name.

Boomer had set up an electronic deposit directly into Molly's bank account in San Francisco. Her money was always available on the first day of each month, so she had little reason to contact either of her parents. She continued to make excuses as to why she was unable to visit them on weekends. When Elizabeth insisted that she come home for

Easter, Molly had said that she wanted to come for a visit and that she would "try really hard" to arrange her study schedule so that she could spend the holiday in Dallas. On Good Friday she called to say that she couldn't make it.

Elizabeth was more worried than she had ever been. She loved Molly so much; all she wanted was for her to have a good life, but Molly was slipping away. She thought that Molly might be avoiding her because of the tension that had existed between the two of them at Christmas, and she tried hard not to let Molly know about her concerns. Whenever they talked, Elizabeth kept the conversation light and upbeat. Most of her e-mails to Molly were funny things that she forwarded, and she avoided asking questions that might make it seem as if she were "prying" into her daughter's life.

As the school year drew to a close, Boomer made arrangements for Molly to work with him at the firm. He had an office cleared for her with a view of some of the most impressive real estate in Dallas. He was excited because his little girl was going to spend the summer putting what she had learned during the past year to practical use. She would have the added advantage of getting some real-life design experience to take back to school in the fall.

Molly arrived in Dallas late in the evening of the first Thursday in June. On Friday Elizabeth told her to put on something pretty because she and her dad had a surprise for her. When Molly was ready, Elizabeth drove her to Bradley Anderson and Associates where Boomer showed her the large corner office that he had prepared for her.

"It's empty!" he beamed. "A blank slate. This will be your first design project—an office for a young professional woman. I want you to put in flooring, wall color, window treatments, furniture, art, and accessories. Whatever you need in the way of carpenters and painters will be provided by our crews. Your budget is thirty thousand dollars. Dazzle me."

Molly looked uncomfortable. "You shouldn't set up anything for me. I'll be leaving soon."

"You'll be going back to school, but you'll need an office this summer, and you'll use it every summer until you graduate. After that it'll be your permanent workplace. No one will use it when you're not here. We'll just shut the door and keep everybody out except the cleaning crew.

Molly barely glanced at the room. It was the kind of space that people work their whole lives to attain, but she did not even walk over to the floor to ceiling windows that covered one wall to look at the view. As an aspiring interior designer, she should have been elated. Instead, she appeared bored and uninterested.

Elizabeth felt her hands go cold and sweaty. Her throat was dry, and a knot formed in the pit of her stomach. Boomer seemed unmoved and continued to smile and show Molly around as if nothing were wrong. She wondered whether Boomer was actually oblivious to Molly's reaction or whether he was simply trying to sell her on her summer job.

After the tour, they took Molly to her favorite restaurant for lunch. She ordered sushi but ate only a bite or two.

When Boomer was half-way through his bacon cheese burger and steak fries, he took a long swig from his Coke and wiped his mouth with his napkin. "I was going to wait until tonight to tell you this, but I can't." He glanced knowingly at Elizabeth as he made the announcement, "We're building a high-rise with thirty-five luxury condos. The building will also house shops, restaurants, a state-of-the-art health club, and a roof-top deck with a pool and outdoor kitchen for the exclusive use of the residents. I've already told Pam that you're going to be working with her on the project this summer as a design assistant." By the time he had finished, Boomer was grinning like a kid on Christmas morning.

"Who's Pam?" Molly asked with little interest.

"Oh, Honey, you remember Pam Greely. She's headed up our interior design team since we first started. She's the one that always sent you and Tracy those little hair do dads she makes out of ribbon."

"Fat Pam? No! I can't stand her."

"She had by-pass surgery; she's skinny Pam now. Besides, Pam's the best interior designer in Dallas, and she's just as sweet and nice as she can be. You be nice to her; I don't want you hurting her feelings."

Molly shrugged and looked at her plate as she pushed a piece of sushi into a bowl of dipping sauce and watched it sink to the bottom.

Since Molly was to begin her job on Monday morning, Elizabeth had made plans for a family outing over the weekend. She announced that on Saturday morning they were all going to their lake house in Austin where they could swim and sail and picnic, just as they had when the girls were little. Molly, however, had other plans. She told Elizabeth that she had already promised some of her friends that she would go to a party they were giving on Saturday night. She encouraged her parents to take Tracy and go without her.

"Molly, Honey, it's a coming-home celebration for you. We're not going without you," Elizabeth responded. "We'll go later in the summer when we can all go together."

"Mom, I wish you wouldn't do this. Don't make plans for me, and don't cancel your plans because of me. I'm a big girl."

Elizabeth felt tears well up in her eyes, but she turned her head so that Molly would not see how hurt she was. "It's okay," she said as she struggled to keep her voice steady.

Chapter 16

On Monday Molly kissed Elizabeth good-by and climbed into her little BMW that her parents had given her for a high school graduation gift. Boomer had left for the office an hour earlier, and she was to join him there at 9:00 A.M.

As Molly sped down the drive, Tracy joined Elizabeth on the porch. "I don't think she's coming back, Mom."

"What are you talking about?"

"Last night after you and Dad went to bed, I heard her out on the porch, and I looked out my window. The doors to her bedroom were open, and she was carrying out her clothes and shoes and putting them in the trunk of her car. I think she's running away."

"Running away? She's nineteen; she's a legal adult; you can't run away at nineteen. Why wouldn't she tell us if she were leaving?"

"She probably knew that you and Dad would try to stop her."

"What did she tell you, Tracy?"

"She didn't tell me anything. She's hardly spoken to me since she arrived on Thursday. Other than a few sarcastic remarks about how I'm a little loser who's never going to have a future because I don't have the guts to take charge of my life, she hasn't said much."

"Why didn't you tell me that you saw her taking her clothes to her car?"

"You just said it, Mom. She's an adult. You can't legally keep her here, and she was going to leave no matter what anyone said. I didn't want her to have the satisfaction of seeing you beg her to stay."

Elizabeth broke into sobs, and Tracy wrapped her arms around her and held her close.

Elizabeth waited until 9:30 to call Boomer to find out whether Molly had arrived at the office. Just as she reached for the phone, it rang.

"Elizabeth, Molly's not here yet. Is everything okay?"

Elizabeth told Boomer everything that she knew. "I was actually reaching for the phone to call you when it rang," she said. "I wanted to give her plenty of time to get to the office, just in case Tracy was wrong."

"Did you argue?" Boomer asked.

"No, she was friendlier than she's been for a long time. She even kissed me good-by. Tracy and I looked in her room to make certain that she really did take everything. It's all gone: her clothes, her shoes, her jewelry."

"She didn't leave anything?"

"She didn't take any of her family pictures or souvenirs. She left everything connected to Tracy and us."

Boomer felt his knees go weak, and he quickly sat down in his heavily padded leather chair. His face had turned the color of ash, and his hands were trembling, "I'm going to make some calls, Lizzie. I'll talk to you later."

Boomer walked to his office door and locked it. Then he rang his secretary on the intercom and told her to hold all of his calls unless they were from Elizabeth or one of his girls.

Boomer's first call was to Dustin, who told him that he and Molly had broken up three months earlier and that she had moved out of their apartment at that time. It took several seconds for Dustin's statement to sink in. "Your apartment? What do you mean?"

"She moved out of our apartment at the end of February. She met some guy at The Bay and moved in with him. I couldn't afford the rent on my allowance so I had to let the loft go and move back on campus."

Boomer was stunned to discover that Molly had been living with Dustin. He knew that she resented their strict rules, but he had always believed that her own Christian convictions would keep her restrained. He would have bet his life that there were certain lines that she would not cross, and living with a man to whom she was not married was one of them.

"What's The Bay?" Boomer asked.

"It's a club in the warehouse district. It's popular with the college kids."

"What's the guy's name?"

"I think it was Mike or Mark or Mack—something like that."

"Is he a student?"

"No, he's some old guy."

"How old?"

"Twenty-nine, thirty. I don't know."

"Do you know where he works?"

"I think he bounces at one of the clubs. I never talked to him."

"Dustin, I want you to know that if I ever see you again I'm going to break your scrawny little neck," and with that Boomer hung up the phone.

Boomer's mobile was beeping to signal that he had received a text message. "Mom & Dad, I lv u. I jst hv 2 B fre. I am OK. Dnt try 2 fnd me. Molly.

Boomer read the message over and over again, and then he laid his head on his desk and cried like a baby.

Chapter 17

James arrived early at the job site. It was his second day as an employee of Ferguson Building Corp., and he did not want to give Billy any reason to complain about him to Judge Chavez. The truth was that James was looking forward to painting Riley's Steak House. Painting was James' one skill, and he had learned to enjoy hours spent quietly applying color to the walls of beautiful buildings. The solitude had sometimes made him feel lonely, but as he had worked the day before priming the walls at Riley's, James had felt a peace and calm that was new to him. He hoped that today he would be able to recapture that feeling.

When he opened the first can of paint and poured it into the tray, he felt himself relax—as if all the tension had drained out of his body. As James painted, he understood why serenity was Billy Ferguson's favorite paint color. It was the color of a winter sky before a storm; it was the color of the ocean at dawn; it was the color of rocks washed smooth by a sparkling stream; it was the color of serenity.

James' mind drifted back to happier days when he was a child and had loved life. He remembered coming in from play and being greeted by the delicious aroma of his mother's cooking; he remembered going camping with his father in the fall when the air had turned cool and crisp; he remembered the sound of logs crackling in the fireplace at Christmas. James was so engrossed in his thoughts that he was unaware that tears were streaming down his cheeks. These were not the bitter tears of anger and pain that he had shed in recent years. These were cleansing tears that bathed his soul and left him feeling renewed.

By 5:45, however, James was mentally planning his weekend. It was Friday and he was trying to decide whether he should risk trying to score some weed. He knew that if Billy Ferguson found out, he would call the judge. Billy was the type who was willing to give a guy a chance, but if James messed up, he wasn't going to cut him any slack. As James pondered his options, Tracer came through the door.

"We're going to CR tonight," Tracer announced. "I'll follow you to the apartment, and we'll leave your car there. You can ride with me."

"What's CR?"

"Celebrate Recovery. Granddad said that you need to get started ASAP."

James still had no idea what Tracer was talking about. "What's Celebrate Recovery?"

"It's a program at our church for people with all sorts of addictions. Some of them have been clean for years, but they're still involved. Most of the leaders are ex-addicts themselves, so they know when someone's trying to mess with their heads."

James felt his throat go dry and his stomach flip-flop. "I'm real tired. I think I'll skip this time."

"Nope," Tracer answered pleasantly. "CR meets every Friday night, and Granddad said that you gotta go."

James' mind was racing. Maybe he could distract Tracer and avoid a Friday night therapy session. "Okay, that's cool. Can we get something to eat first? I'm starved."

"We'll eat at the church. Tonight's spaghetti night. In fact, every Friday night's spaghetti night."

At the mention of spaghetti, James perked up a little. His mom was third generation Italian, and she had learned to cook from her Italian mother and grandmother. Just the thought of a pot of her spaghetti sauce simmering on the stove made his mouth water. In his memory he could smell the rich tomato sauce laced with fresh basil, garlic, and oregano; he could almost taste the freshly grated parmesan and the crusty bread hot from the oven.

James was unaware that he was about to encounter something far more frightening than a Celebrate Recovery meeting every Friday night. He was about to be introduced to a diet of church spaghetti every Friday night.

When they arrived at San Antonio Believers Church, James was relieved to see that there were not many cars in the parking lot. Maybe they would send everyone home. James had once seen a sign that read, "Due to a lack of interest, today has been cancelled." Maybe due to a lack of interest, CR would be cancelled.

When he and Tracer entered the fellowship hall, however, James saw that it was nearly full. People were eating at the various folding tables covered with paper tablecloths, and there was still a line at the kitchen pass through window.

Tracer motioned for James to get in line ahead of him, and as he stood observing the crowd, he noticed that almost everyone there looked "normal". "They're probably the guards," James thought. He was able to pick out two or three who looked as if they might be in recovery, but most of them looked like church Nazis who wanted to force everyone to live like they did.

When James reached the window, a smiling woman of about forty greeted him warmly, and handed him a plate. Without responding James took the soggy looking paper plate and the small paper napkin wrapped around a plastic fork and spoon and walked to the nearest table. Tracer was right behind him.

"Let's get some tea," Tracer said.

The two of them walked to the large aluminum drink dispenser and filled their Styrofoam cups with iced tea.

When he was seated, James tasted the tea. It was unsweetened and watery. Barely cool and with no visible signs of ice, it hardly qualified as iced tea. As James swallowed he surveyed his plate. Even before he tasted the mound of sticky pasta covered with a lukewarm sauce comprised solely of a minimal amount of ground beef and a large quantity of bottled spaghetti sauce, James knew that this was not an authentic Italian meal. He picked up the roll that had been served straight from the package with no preparation.

To his surprise, James saw that people were eating the food as if it were delicious. Before he had finished a third of his meal, Tracer had cleaned his plate and gone back for seconds.

Tracer was watching James closely. When he was nearly finished, Tracer asked if he would like some more. "No, I'm good!" James said, trying to sound up beat.

"Okay. I'll get our dessert."

Tracer returned with two small paper plates with a square of milky-looking lime Jell-O in the center of each. James was certain that the top layer contained cottage cheese, and he nearly gagged. James ignored the plate that Tracer had set before him, but Tracer downed his Jell-O in three bites.

"Are you gonna eat that?" Tracer asked motioning toward the Jell-O.

"Help yourself," James replied, and Tracer smiled broadly as he pulled James' plate in front of him.

When the meal had ended and the tables and chairs had been folded and stacked against a wall, a short, balding man of about fifty announced that everyone should go into his group.

"If you're new here," the man continued, "you're in luck! We just started our new groups last week, so you can still get in. If you haven't been assigned to a group yet, come on over and talk to me."

James stood perfectly still until Tracer nudged him in the back. Both boys moved toward the speaker, and Tracer made introductions. "Tony, this is James Goodwin. He just got out of rehab two days ago and needs some good fellowship. James, this is Tony Manzo. Tony's the men's leader, and he's gonna get you put into the right group."

James wasn't listening. He had spotted a pretty young woman of about nineteen with red curly hair and dimples. She was talking to the women's leader, but she looked very unhappy about being there. James was pretty sure that, if he played his cards right, he could hook up with her.

Tony's voice interrupted James' thoughts. "You come with me, James."

James turned to see Tracer exiting the room. "Isn't he coming with me?"

"Everything said in our groups is strictly confidential. We restrict each group to six or seven people, and we never allow anyone to sit in who's not part of the group."

James was disappointed to see that the red-haired girl was walking with the women's leader in the opposite direction. Tony noticed James' interest and said, "Our groups are segregated. This is not a dating service."

"I've taken a liking to you," Tony continued as he smiled at James and put his arm around his shoulder. "I'm putting you in the group that I teach."

"Of course, you are," James thought. "I can't catch a break. You guys won't give me room to breathe."

Tony guided James into a small Sunday school room with eight metal folding chairs arranged in a circle. Tony sat in one of the two empty seats, and James took the other.

"Welcome to CR!" Tony began in a booming voice. "Who was here last week?" Three hands attached to three tired-looking men ranging in age from thirty to forty-five went up.

"Okay," Tony continued. "So, we have four new members tonight, and I'm closing our group. It usually takes several weeks to reach capacity, but this time we managed to do it in two weeks. Let's give God a big hand-clap for bringing everybody in so quickly!"

Everyone except James applauded. "I don't believe this. I'm a prisoner in a group led by the mayor of Crazy Town!" he thought.

Tony introduced himself to the group and then had each man introduce himself and tell "in twenty-five words or less" why he was there. When it was James' turn, he was tempted to blurt out, "I'm here because I've been kidnapped by a crazy judge, a weird old builder, and some hick kid who are making me nuts. I didn't need therapy until I met them; now I may never be able to regain my sanity!" Instead, he looked at the floor as he mumbled, "I just got out of drug rehab, and I need to make sure that I stay clean."

When the introductions were finished, Tony said, "I'm going to give you a little background on Celebrate Recovery. It was started in 1991 by John Baker, a pastor at Saddleback Church where Rick Warren is the senior pastor. Anyone here who doesn't know who Rick Warren is?"

James had never heard of Rick Warren, but he wasn't about to admit it, and he continued to sit staring at the floor with his arms folded tightly across his chest.

"Well," Tony continued, "John Baker modeled Celebrate Recovery after the twelve-step recovery program that Alcoholics Anonymous developed, but it's not affiliated with AA, and at CR we deal with every kind of addiction you can think of: alcohol, drugs, gambling, pornography, overeating, shopping, and hoarding. There's probably a lot more, but that's the only ones I can think of off the top of my head. Our purpose is to help people get free of their hurts, hang-ups, and habits.

"CR is based on the eight principles of the Beatitudes—also known as the Sermon on the Mount—found in Matthew 5:3-10. I'm gonna go over all eight real quick for you because in the following weeks we're gonna be talking about them a lot.

"*First,* I realize that I am not God. I am powerless to control my tendency to do the wrong things.

"*Second,* I earnestly believe that God exists and that I matter to Him. I believe that He has the power to help me recover.

"*Third,* I consciously choose to commit all my life and will to Jesus Christ's care and control.

"*Fourth,* I openly examine and confess my faults to God, to myself, and to someone I trust.

"*Fifth,* I voluntarily submit to every change God wants to make in my life, and I ask Him to remove my character defects.

"*Sixth,* I evaluate all my relationships. I forgive all those who have hurt me, and I make amends for harm I've done to others—except when to do so would harm them or others.

"*Seventh,* I reserve a time with God each day for self-examination, Bible reading, and prayer.

"*Eighth,* I yield myself to God to be used to bring His Good News to others, both by my example and my words."

Tony then talked about his own relationship with Christ. He did not give a personal testimony; his remarks centered on the saving power of Jesus and the way that having a relationship with Christ had changed his life and given him back his family at a time when his wife had left him.

Tony was genuine—James could see that. He loved Jesus, and he wanted to help these men know Him the way he did. James relaxed a little and unfolded his arms. He had no intentions of buying into this CR stuff, but he liked Tony. "Before he got into all this Jesus stuff," James thought, "he was probably a cool guy."

At 9:00 P.M. Tony announced, "We're out of time for tonight. Next week we'll get down to work. We'll be talking about things here that we may never have told anyone else. I want to caution you right now. What happens in CR, stays in CR! We keep our groups small and close them within a few weeks because we get to know each other and build relationships. I don't want to ever hear of any of you talking about anything that is said in this group to anyone outside the group. Does everybody understand?"

When the session ended, Tracer was waiting outside the door of James' room.

"How'd it go?" Tracer asked.

"We're not allowed to talk about it," James answered smugly, and he felt a tiny sense of victory over Tracer.

"You been here all this time?" James added.

"Not here, here. I was in the sanctuary practicing for Sunday morning."

"Practicing what?"

"I play the guitar for praise and worship. You'll like the praise and worship; it's great!"

James had just spent two hours listening to six losers talk about how they had gotten clean and gotten saved. They were struggling, but they had finished the week without falling back into their old habits. No one had used drugs or alcohol or looked at porn or beaten up his wife and kids. It was enough to cause James to run screaming and jump headfirst through the nearest window. If the broken shards of glass should decapitate him in the process, so much the better.

It was late; James was tired, and his nerves were shot. Tracer had just implied that James was expected to attend church on Sunday. He was not going to allow this to go any farther.

"Am I required to go to church?" he asked coldly.

"Course not!" Tracer replied enthusiastically. "Nobody can make you go to church. That's gotta be your decision."

James was silent during the drive back to his apartment. As soon as Tracer stopped his truck, James had the door open and was out. Tracer rolled down his window and blew the horn. When James turned back toward the truck he saw Tracer's big smiling face. "Hey, Jimbo, I'll pick you up Sunday morning at 8:30. Be ready to go!" With his truck radio blaring Christian music from a local station, Tracer drove away.

Chapter 18

On Saturday James slept late and then strolled around the apartment complex. When he came to the deserted pool, he sat down on the edge and dangled his feet in the cold water. He thought about his situation for a long time and finally decided that he could not afford to risk violating his probation. As the owner of the complex, Billy Ferguson had keys to his apartment and could enter it whenever he wished. If he should discover alcohol or drugs there he would call Judge Chavez, and James would go directly to jail.

The sun glared off the water and hurt James' eyes. He felt as if he were being punished by the court, by his employer, and by Tracer. "I hate all of them," he thought.

After several minutes, however, James made a decision. He would go to work every day and do the best job of which he was capable. He would be courteous and helpful and would go far beyond what was expected of him. He would be on time for his appointments with his probation officer, and he would tell him everything that he wanted to hear. He would attend CR and eat that nasty spaghetti as if it were manna from heaven. He would participate and appear to be enthusiastic about the program. For the next year he would be a model citizen; he would play the part of the poor kid who got addicted to pain killers when he had an unfortunate accident and was now working to get his life straightened out.

"When that year is up," James said out loud, "I'm going to get into the Focus and drive until I get so far away from this place that I can't even remember the way back."

Having settled how he would spend the next twelve months, James spent the rest of the day lying around his apartment staring at the ceiling.

James was up early on Sunday. He showered, shaved, and made himself look as presentable as possible. He had imagined what he would say when Tracer arrived to pick him up. He was prepared to really spread it on thick and talk about how much he had enjoyed CR. When he heard Tracer's truck horn blaring, he jumped to his feet and opened the door. As he stepped into the parking lot, however, he stopped dead in his tracks. Sitting beside Tracer on the bench seat of the old Ford Truck was the red-haired girl from CR. She was all smiles, and her red curls bounced as she moved her head in time with the music that was playing on the radio.

As James opened the truck door, Tracer smiled broadly and said, "Hey, Jimbo, are you ready for the best praise and worship in Texas!"

James immediately forgot everything he had planned to say and silently climbed into the cab beside the red-haired girl.

"This here's Macy," Tracer said. "She's the best keyboard player you ever saw! Wait till you hear her cut loose."

James managed to recover himself enough to ask, "Are you in CR too?"

"Oh, heck no!" Macy replied, showing even white teeth as her beautiful pink lips curved into a smile.

"I thought I saw you there on Friday," James replied.

"I was there. There's a girl at school that's been having a lot of trouble since her parents got divorced. I finally talked her into getting into the women's group. I practiced with the band while she was in CR."

"Jimbo, do you play?" Tracer asked.

"Sure. I played for a while in a band in LA."

That wasn't exactly true. Shirley's boyfriend had played in a band and he had sometimes allowed James to sit in on the practice sessions and play along with them, but James had never been part of the band or played any of their club dates.

"You play guitar?" Tracer inquired.

"Sure do."

"You want to join the band? We can always use more musicians," Macy asked.

"Absolutely," James responded. This was working out better than he had anticipated. He was going to have an excuse to spend some quality time with Macy, and he was sure that with his good looks and charm he would win her over in no time.

Chapter 19

The young woman was weaving her way through the tightly-packed tables. With her four-inch stiletto heels and a tray of drinks balanced in her right hand, it was no easy task. Yet, she moved quickly and gracefully, and as she passed each table the eyes of the male customers locked on her and followed her journey to the far end of the room.

"Hey, Andi," called a dissipated-looking forty-year old sitting at a table with three guys from his office. "Come over here and sit on my lap."

The young woman turned and smiled in his direction. Placing the drinks on the table, she made her way toward him. "Artie, it's about time you said something. I thought you were ignoring me," she purred. "You got a fifty?"

Artie produced the fifty-dollar bill, which the young woman deposited into her push-up bra as she wiggled her way onto his lap. "I missed you, Honey," she said seductively and then gave him a big kiss on the side of his face. The other three guys at the table looked impressed.

"Gotta get back to work," Andi whispered in his ear as she slid off his lap and picked up her empty tray.

All of the Cocktails wore identical black mini skirts, black low-cut tank tops, and outlandish hot pink wigs styled in a puffy bob. At first glance, they appeared to be clones of one another, but on closer examination it was evident that Andi was a little different from the others. Although she was more overtly sexual than most of the Cocktails, there was an underlying current of refinement that seemed to contradict her present circumstances. Her long shapely legs were bare and sported a spray-on tan rather than the fish-net stockings that most of the other Cocktails preferred. Her perfume was subtle and expensive and guaranteed to go straight to a man's head. It was clear that Andi had not been part of the club scene for long.

As the young woman returned to the bar to pick up another tray of drinks, the head bouncer's hand shot out and grabbed her by the wrist. "What were you doing over there, Molly?"

The young woman reached inside her bra and showed Matt the corner of the fifty she had just deposited there. Then she smiled and winked as she walked away with hips swaying and the pink bob bouncing lightly.

When Molly had left Dallas to return to San Francisco, she was afraid that her parents would try to find her. She imagined that they might kidnap her and forcibly return her to Dallas. In her fantasy she envisioned being somewhere and having someone speak her name within earshot of her parents. They would then turn and spot her before she could get away.

To prevent that from happening, she had taken a "professional name". All of her employment records listed her as Molly Anderson, but to the customers and other club employees she was known as Andi Maguire. Andi she took from Anderson and Maguire was a nod to the Molly Maguires that she had heard Boomer talk about when she was a little girl. Stories of the secret society of Irish-Americans that were active in the Pennsylvania coal fields from the time of the Civil War until the late 1870s had always fascinated Molly, and she had sometimes imagined that one day she would change her name to Molly Maguire. Now, in her attempt to remain anonymous, she had almost achieved that goal.

At work, Molly was all smiles and bravado; anyone would have thought that she was teeming with confidence. In truth, she was disappointed with the way things were turning out. When she had left Dallas two months earlier, she had expected to spend the summer partying. Matt had bragged about all the money he made bouncing at *Pink*, and she had not doubted that he was telling her the truth. The money that Boomer automatically deposited into her account each month had paid for their apartment and other living expenses, but she had assumed that Matt had a nice bank roll stashed away somewhere.

On the day that she had left Dallas, however, Boomer had cancelled the automatic deposits, and by July 1 her account was nearly empty. A few days later Matt came home from work with a "uniform" for her. As she picked up the black mini and tank top and examined the fluffy pink wig, she knew that she was not going to be able to play the part of the pampered little rich girl any longer.

"What's this?" she asked, holding the pink bob up high in her right hand.

"It's your new do, Baby," Matt answered carelessly. "Why do you think they call the club *Pink*?"

Molly had begun her new career the following day. She spent her evenings carrying drinks to obnoxious customers, and when the club closed at 2:30 A.M., she had to help the other Cocktails clear the tables, clean the bathrooms, and sweep and mop the floors. All of the girls changed into tennis shoes and pulled off their wigs for the clean-up. They were a sad sight, cleaning the drafty former warehouse in the middle of the night. As Molly and the other Cocktails labored, she could not help remembering the scene from *Annie* where Miss Hannigan punishes the orphans by forcing them to spend the night scrubbing the orphanage until it shone "like the top of the Chrysler Building." She was even tempted to break into a chorus of *It's a Hard Knock Life*.

Molly was already tired of Matt. His ex-wife had dropped his two kids off at their apartment the first Saturday after she had returned from Dallas. The boys, ages four and six, were classic brats. Molly had never liked children, and Matt's kids were not going to be the ones to change her mind. Matt, however, expected her to keep them entertained while he watched television and drank beer.

Thirty minutes into the boys' visit Molly picked up her purse and the keys to her BMW and, without a word, walked out the door. She called Dustin, who was not particularly enthusiastic about hearing from her but finally agreed to meet her at Starbucks. From there they went back to his apartment, got high, and ended up in bed together.

When Molly returned to her apartment around noon on Sunday, Matt was furious. "Where have you been?" he shouted. "Madrid was ready to fire you last night. I told him that you had food poisoning to keep you from getting canned!"

Ignoring him, she walked to the bedroom and shut the door. She showered, oiled her long tan legs, put on her make-up, and dressed for work. When she was ready, she left the apartment without ever speaking to or looking at Matt.

After that, Matt's kids did not come to the apartment, but Molly was sick and tired of his temper tantrums and constant demands. For the past several weeks she had been plotting her departure from San Francisco, and when Julie was hired as a Cocktail, Molly saw her plans come together.

Madrid, *Pink's* owner, had hired Julie as a favor to her mother. Angela was his live-in girlfriend, and Madrid considered her something of a trophy. Angela had worked as a stripper at *The Purple Parrot* until she met Madrid a year earlier and had talked him into setting her up in a modeling and talent agency. It was a perfect transition for a still-beautiful woman whose charm and sex appeal would continue to work in her favor for the next few years. Angela had to admit, however, that when a woman is on the wrong side of thirty she has to start pursuing career options that do not include a pole and a feather boa. Her agency allowed her to exploit good-looking kids who dreamed of becoming super models and movie stars. She was the perfect spokeswoman for a stable of "talent" that she could pimp out for hefty fees to the wealthy businessmen that abounded in San Francisco.

Angela had given birth to Julie when she was only fifteen, and now, at age thirty-three, she had an eighteen year-old daughter who needed a job. Julie was something of an embarrassment to Angela, both because of her appearance and because having a grown daughter made her feel old. Julie was short and thick with bowed legs and a neck that looked like it belonged on a wrestler. Her lower arms were covered in fine black hair, and a soft roll of fat showed through the tank top of her Cocktail uniform. When Julie dressed for her first day of work at *Pink*, Angela shuddered.

"You look beautiful, Baby," Angela called. Sadly, Julie believed her and, with her hot pink bob pushed firmly down on her head, she left for the club.

As soon as Julie walked through the door, Molly zeroed in on her and began laying the groundwork for her plan. Molly knew at once that she could easily manipulate Julie into sharing an apartment with her and paying most of the expenses. Julie would also do all of the laundry and cooking, and if they ran short of money, she could always get some help from her mom. Julie was flattered that the most beautiful girl at *Pink* would want to be her friend, and within a couple of weeks she was agreeing to everything Molly suggested.

Saturday, September 15, was Matt's twenty-eighth birthday. When he was ready to leave for work at the club, he was surprised to see that Molly was still wearing her white shorts and yellow halter top.

"Come on, Babe. Get a move on," he said to Molly.

"It's your birthday," Molly responded in her most suggestive manner. "I'm taking the day off to get a big surprise ready for you when you get home tonight. I had to wait until I got paid yesterday to get your gift."

"Does Madrid know you're not coming in?"

"Of course, I cleared it with him. Don't be late, Baby, because what I have planned is guaranteed to knock your socks off!"

As soon as Matt left Molly pulled her suitcases out from under the bed. She had already packed most of her belongings, and it took only a few minutes to put in the rest. She carried her bags to the BMW and put them into the trunk. Returning to the apartment, she picked up her purse, threw the spare key onto the kitchen counter and said to the empty rooms, "Bye-bye, sucker. Hope this is a big enough surprise to make your birthday really memorable."

Closing the apartment door after her, Molly climbed into her car, picked up Julie, who was waiting for her outside her mom's apartment, and headed for Los Angeles.

Chapter 20

By early October James was more than half-way through his probation. He had always thought of himself as a cool guy who happened to have been born to two very uncool parents, and he had spent every day since he had turned thirteen working to prove just how cool he was. Being cool was hard work, and for a guy like James, to whom being cool did not come naturally, all that coolness took a toll.

For the past few months, however, James had been required to be hard-working and respectful. In addition, he was forced to pretend to be interested in CR and in turning his life around. He would never have admitted it to himself, but James found the demands of his new life easier than the pressures of his old one. When one plays a part for a long enough time, he begins to convince himself that he is the character he pretends to be, and James was being influenced by his new persona far more than he would have liked to admit.

During his second CR meeting Tony Manzo had told the group that a good way to remember the Beatitudes is to say, "These are the *attitudes* that I want to *be* in my life." James had found that phrase very irritating, and exactly because he found it so irritating, he decided to make a big deal of pretending that it was his special connection with CR.

James was playing a role, and the more he got into it, the more he enjoyed playing it. Whenever Tony referred to one of the Beatitudes, James would throw his hands into the air and exclaim, "These are the attitudes that I want to be in my life!" This declaration would be followed by smiles and choruses of "Amen!" from the other members of the group. At those times, James felt in control, and he experienced a rush that he had seldom known.

Just as James thought that he had pretty much gotten the CR thing down pat, however, a strange thing happened. One Friday evening the group was discussing the precept, *I consciously choose to commit all my life and will to Christ's care and control*, and James, as usual, threw his hands into the air and declared, "That's an attitude that I want to be in my life!"

Instantly, he felt tears well up in his eyes, and he was engulfed with a sense of shame. To his horror, the tears began to course down his cheeks, and he felt his entire body tremble. Every eye was fastened on him as he began to sob. As the sobs grew louder, Tony came over to him and put his arms around him. The other men began to pray for him that God would help him fully commit his life to Christ and to overcome anything that was holding him back.

Tony knew that this was the first genuine thing that James had done during several months of CR meetings. He had not said anything to James about his lack of sincerity, but he had not been fooled by him either. Tony had liked James from the moment he had met him, and even though he knew full well that James was a deceitful little punk, Tony saw something in him that made him believe that James would one day become a true man of God. Tony had prayed for James regularly and waited for God to move in his life.

James drove back to his apartment with tears still streaming down his cheeks. He was embarrassed that he could not stop the flow of tears, but once the floodgates had been opened, they would not close again until the cleansing process was complete.

As soon as he was inside, he went to the bedroom and picked up the Bible that Tracer had given him after the first CR meeting. He had never opened it, but now he turned to Chapter 1 of Genesis and began reading: "When God began creating the heavens and the earth, the earth was at first a shapeless, chaotic mass, with the Spirit of God brooding over the dark vapors."

James had heard the words before. When he was a child in Sunday school this was among the scripture verses he had memorized. Although the words were familiar, however, he read them as if he were seeing them for the first time. They leapt off the page and landed in his heart. On and on he read, taking in verse after verse as a man held under water for a long time gasps for air when he finally reaches the surface.

What he had always believed to be dead and dry had in a single moment become a spring of life-giving water that filled him with joy and peace. James stopped reading and began praying; he thanked God for sending him to San Antonio, and he thanked God for Judge Chavez, and Billy Ferguson, and Tracer. He thanked God for his accident and for getting arrested, and for everything in his life that had led him to this moment.

"Oh, Jesus!" he cried, "Please forgive me for my sins. I want to know you, and I want to serve you. Help me to become the man you created me to be." On and on he prayed, talking to Jesus as if he were his older brother, his best friend, his God, and his Savior.

After a long time he realized that it was growing light, and when he glanced at the digital clock on the bedside table, he saw that it was 6:00 A.M. Still clutching his Bible, he slid down on the pillows and closed his eyes.

When James awoke, it was 1:30. The praise and worship band was meeting at 2:00 to discuss the songs for Sunday's service and have a practice session. Grabbing a can of Coke from the refrigerator, he splashed water on his face, picked up his keys, and headed out the door.

James had joined the praise and worship band the week after he had begun attending CR. It was the first time he had ever been able to perform on stage, and he loved it. Each week as he stood before the congregation playing the guitar that Tracer had loaned him and singing the lyrics to the choruses, he imagined that he was a rock star. He had been forced to stay for the preaching afterwards, but he had managed to tune out the pastor's message. If anyone could have looked inside his head during the service, they would have seen the greatest rocker the world has ever known screaming out his songs on a stage surrounded by beautiful scantily-clad women and rough-looking band members. As the lights flashed and the smoke rose from the stage, the audience of thousands rose to their feet, swaying to the throb of the music as they cheered wildly and called his name.

James arrived at the church just as the band was beginning to play. Clutching his guitar, he jumped onto the stage and took his place alongside Tracer. For the first time since he had joined the praise and worship team, as the band began playing, James was not transported to a rock star fantasy. He had been singing the choruses for months, but now they were no longer someone else's words set to someone else's music. He took ownership of those choruses, and they became his soul's cry to Jesus Christ, his personal praise for God's only Son who had died for his sins and set him free.

On and on the team sang: "We are redeemed, we are forgiven..." "Every knee shall bow, and every tongue confess, that Jesus Christ is Lord..." "Our God is an awesome God; He reigns from Heaven above..." "Hallelujah! Grace like rain falls down on me..." James was no longer the rock star of his own private universe. He had been transported from an unrepentant sinner to a child of God washed clean by the blood of Jesus, and he was scarcely able to comprehend the joy that flooded his soul.

Chapter 21

The next few months were the hardest James had ever experienced. When he had been only pretending to want to turn his life around, he was simply playing a part. He was the clever manipulator making fools of everyone who believed that he was sincere.

When he accepted Jesus, however, the change became real. His commitment was permanent, and he could no longer look forward to the day when he would drive off into the sunset and never look back. Suddenly, his efforts to remain clean and sober became much more of a struggle. He could never again use drugs or alcohol. He could no longer lie to and manipulate others. The prospect of having to live his life in an honest and straight-forward manner was terrifying.

James knew that if he were to succeed, he would need CR more than ever. Until he had accepted Jesus, he had used CR as a prop to help him play out his part. Now he attended the meetings to reinforce his commitment to his new life. He sincerely shared his fears, his temptations, his triumphs, his hopes, and his dreams with the other members. Those Friday night meetings became a lifeline that kept him firmly anchored to his new life.

On the Sunday morning after James accepted Jesus Tony Manzo pulled him aside after the church service to talk to him. James told Tony everything, and Tony looked thoughtful. Finally, he said, "I have an assignment for you, James. I want you to read the four Gospels straight through three times during the next thirty days. When you're finished, you'll know what to do."

"How will I know, man?"

"Trust me. You'll know."

James was thrilled. Was this like a message from God? He wanted to ask Tony, but he was unwilling to risk having Tony tell him that it was not God's message for him; it was Tony's. James remained quiet until he realized that he had no idea what Tony was talking about.

"Uh, what are the four Gospels?"

"They're the first four books of the New Testament—Matthew, Mark, Luke, and John."

"Are they long?"

"Not very, James. You can do it, but make sure you finish before the thirty days are up."

"Okay, right, yeah, yeah, I will."

James was excited. Who was going to tell him what he was supposed to do? Was God going to send an angel to him? Was he going to suddenly find himself famous? Was a record producer going to offer him a recording contract? The possibilities were endless, but this much James knew for certain: Whatever it was, it was going to be big!

That afternoon James began his reading assignment. He read with a determination and purpose that he had never given to any undertaking, and he was immediately struck by how interesting and relevant the Gospels were. As the days passed, he was surprised to learn that the four books contained many of the same accounts told from a slightly different perspective. While none of them contradicted the others, each gave information that complemented the other accounts so that the reader was able to gain a much fuller picture of the events that had taken place.

The thirty days passed quickly. James had finished his reading two days earlier, and on the thirtieth day he could hardly contain himself. When he went to work that morning, he had a hard time concentrating on his painting. Billy had sent him to a custom home he was building on a tree studded hill five miles outside of San Antonio. A gentle breeze was blowing the cool air through the open doors of the house as James worked. He was alone at the site, and the only sound was the whisper of the breeze flowing through the branches of the willow tree that the owner had planted a couple of months earlier.

At 1:00 James stopped working to eat the peanut butter and grape jelly sandwich he had brought. He leaned back with his head against the wall and closed his eyes hoping that God would choose this moment to reveal his destiny to him, but the only sound was the breeze as it passed through the branches of the willow.

By the time James had returned to his apartment it was dark. He was disappointed because nothing out of the ordinary had happened. He pulled out his pocket calendar and counted the days again—just to make certain that this was actually day thirty. No doubt about it. This was the day.

James showered, ate a frozen dinner that he heated in the microwave, and waited. The clock read 11:55 P.M. The day was almost over. James was bitterly disappointed, and in desperation he called out, "God! What am I supposed to do?"

Immediately a thought came into his mind. He did not hear a voice, but it was as clear as if it had been spoken, "Keep reading."

James was stunned! That's what he was supposed to do? Keep reading? God didn't have something great for him to do? No angel was going to pay him a visit? God just wanted him to keep on painting and reading the Bible?

"Is that it?" James asked aloud. "I'm just supposed to keep reading?"

Again a crystal clear thought came into James' mind, "I also want you to pay your dad the money you owe him."

Chapter 22

ames was faithful to read the Bible every day. It was not difficult; the more he read, the more he wanted to read. Soon he began sharing what he read with the other guys on the construction crew. Tracer and two others were Christians, but most of them thought that he was "weird," and soon Benson, who was fortyish and had worked for Billy longer than anyone except Tracer, nicknamed him "The Preacher."

James had always hated nicknames. Jimmy and Jiminy were the two from his childhood, and Jimbo, the name Tracer had given him, was no better. The Preacher, however, had a certain ring to it. James liked it. Whenever Benson called him The Preacher, James felt as if someday he might actually be a preacher.

James was also working to get past the feelings of guilt that were eating at him. He felt both sorry and ashamed when he thought of how he had used his parents, but that was over and done with. He had changed; that should be enough. When he told Tracer and Macy about what he had done, he asked them, "Why do I feel so guilty?"

Macy had looked surprised, and opening her green eyes wide, she had exclaimed, "Because you are!"

It seemed to James that Macy was the one person who could always throw him a curve. When he had seen her at that first CR meeting, he had been certain that he would be able to dazzle her with his charm, but he had discovered the next day that she had been "going out" with Tracer since they were sixteen. Macy was bubbling over with excitement the day she told him that she and Tracer were planning their wedding for the following June. She never suspected that her words had hit James like a sack of bricks.

James had hoped that his two friends would offer him some sympathy concerning the way he had treated his parents. After all, he had been suffering horribly when he talked his father into getting him the marijuana. He had hoped that they would tell him that anyone would have done the same in those circumstances and that God understood.

Instead, Macy had looked directly into his eyes and said, "You have to make this right. First, you need to ask Jesus to forgive you, and then you need to make things right with your mom and dad."

James had spent very little money since he had begun working for Billy Ferguson, and he had saved a couple of thousand dollars toward the day when he would escape San Antonio. Now everything had changed, and James knew that he would be staying after he finished his probation. That day he began working to save the rest of the money he would need to make restitution to his parents. He calculated that with the twenty-five hundred dollars his dad had spent for the Focus and the money he had spent getting him the marijuana, James owed his dad forty-eight hundred dollars.

He decided that he would give his dad five thousand dollars and ask for his forgiveness.

James spent the next few months working, going to church, attending CR, and witnessing to everyone he could get to listen. One day when he and Benson were working together James was telling Benson about Jesus. He was sharing scripture and relating all the things that were happening with the praise and worship band. Just as he started making a pitch for Benson to come to church on Sunday, however, Benson changed the subject.

Benson began boasting about how he was the only one working at Ferguson Building Corp. who wasn't afraid of Billy. "He's got all the rest of you scared like you was a bunch of little girls," he taunted, "but he knows better than to get in my face. I tell him what I think, and I can do anything I want because, truth is, the old man can't run this place without me."

As Benson talked, James saw Billy walking toward them. Benson was turned so that he could not see Billy's approach, but James had a clear view. He was trying to decide whether he should warn Benson before Billy got close enough to hear his rant when Billy yelled, "Benson! I need you at the other site! Leave this for James to finish!"

Billy was not angry, but he had a voice like thunder mixed with gravel. Benson nearly jumped out of his skin, and the blood drained from his face. James guffawed.

"What's so funny?" Billy asked with his characteristic broad smile spreading across his face.

"Nothing," James answered. "I was just thinking that God really does have a sense of humor."

Billy patted James' shoulder and walked away as Benson scrambled to pick up the roller he had dropped and put the cover on his paint can.

Chapter 23

Eighteen months after James left his parents' house to return to Angel Fire, he had the five thousand dollars saved. He had not contacted his parents since he left because he did not want to explain to them where he was or what he was doing. On each of their birthdays he had come very near to making a call, but he feared that if he talked to them they would somehow know that he had been arrested and was on probation. It was easier not to have any contact with them until he had finished his probation.

Now James was a free man. He had paid his debt to society, and he was about to pay his debt to his parents. After a number of talks with Tracer and Macy and lots of advice from Tony and the members of his CR group, James had come to the conclusion that he would arrive at his parents' house unannounced, tell them everything that had happened, give his father the cashier's check that he had purchased, and leave.

Although the distance from San Antonio to Ft. Worth is only about four hours by car, James felt that he had embarked on a trip of a million miles. He was not traveling across three hundred miles of asphalt; he was traveling across time. He was going home again—not as the angry young man who wanted nothing more than to put as much distance as possible between his parents and him—but as a prodigal son who had never given a thought to the heartbreak that he had caused them until he had given his life to Jesus.

It was a few minutes before 6:00 P.M. when James arrived at his parents' house. From his chair near the window, his dad saw the car pull up to the curb, but he did not pay it any attention. Barbara answered his knock at the door, and for a few seconds stood staring at him without recognition. Then her face lit up, and she opened the screen door and threw her arms around him.

"Jimmy! What are you doing here? Why didn't you tell us you were coming? Look at you! You look so handsome! John Wesley, come here! Jimmy's come home." Barbara hugged him tightly and then pulled back to look at him before hugging him again.

John Wesley had arrived at the door and was smiling. He gave James a hug and invited him into the house. "We've been worried about you, son. You've been gone a long time."

"I know. I need to talk to you and Mom."

"Let's eat while you talk," Barbara suggested. "I've got dinner ready to take off the stove."

"Let's talk first," James replied. "We'll eat afterwards."

While Barbara took dinner off the stove, James followed John Wesley into the den. It was a small brown room that had changed very little since James was a child. John Wesley settled himself into his recliner, and James sat on the couch.

James began his story with the day he had left this house eighteen months earlier. He told them about seeing Grady in handcuffs and getting arrested himself when he was entering San Antonio. He was completely honest with them, but he did not tell them everything. He would never tell them about his plan to commit suicide, and he would never let them know how angry he had been at them for most of his life.

Just before James had left to see his parents Tony had taken him aside and told him, "Being completely honest doesn't mean that you tell someone everything; it means that you are totally honest about the things you do tell them. Usually, it's better not to get into things that will cause them hurt. That's where Beatitude number six comes in; you make amends for harm you've done to them, but you don't hurt them any further in the process."

James told them that he was sorry for what he had put them through with his accident and for having them get him the marijuana. He asked for their forgiveness and presented John Wesley with the cashier's check.

"No, son." John Wesley said. "We don't want you to pay us back. We're just glad that you're okay."

"Dad, this is important; it's something that I have to do. If you won't take the money for your sake, take it for mine."

John Wesley nodded and laid the check on the end table next to his chair.

James spent the following two days with his parents. It was a good visit. He watched televised sports with his father and sat in the kitchen and talked to his mother while she cooked. He reminded his mother of the promise that he had made her to never use drugs again after his injuries healed, and he told her that even though he had broken that promise, he was renewing it. "This time," he said, "I'll keep it."

The morning that James returned to San Antonio John Wesley told Barbara that he had never believed that James would ever change.

"Jimmy's always been a good boy," Barbara had responded.

"No," John Wesley corrected her. "James was never a good boy. He spent his whole life getting into trouble. If I hadn't been here to see him with my own eyes, I would never believe that he has grown into a decent human being."

"I think you were always too hard on him," Barbara retorted.

"I probably wasn't hard enough on him, but there's no point in arguing about that now. The old James would never have paid back that money. I don't care about the money; I told him that, but the fact that he paid it back tells me that he's changed."

"Well," Barbara said, "I'm afraid that Jimmy has gotten tied up with some religious fanatics. I didn't like some of the things he told me about going to that group for addicts. Jimmy was never an addict. I think he's just growing up. When people grow up, they start acting better; that's all it is."

"You're wrong," John Wesley responded. "James said that he found God, and even though I don't understand what he was talking about, I know it's real to him. I wouldn't want that for myself, but I've seen the change in James, and I know that it's more than just growing up."

Chapter 24

*I*n the spring of 2015 Boomer received a call from Cuatro Bennett who told him that he represented a consortium of Texas businessmen that wanted to build luxury hotels in the major Texas cities. The Texas Grand Hotel Group would build its first hotel in San Antonio and then move on to Austin, Dallas, Ft. Worth, Houston, and Galveston, and they wanted Boomer to be the architect and builder.

Boomer had met Cuatro ten years earlier when he had been invited by a friend to attend the annual conference of the Texas Christian Ranchers Association which was held in Dallas the last week of March each year. The association had begun as an opportunity for Christian ranchers to come together once a year for prayer and fellowship, but by the time Boomer attended, the focus had changed. In addition to the ranchers, businessmen, doctors, attorneys, school teachers, and housewives flocked to the meetings to attend workshops and worship led by some of the most respected Christian leaders in the country. Everyone was welcome, and many lives were changed because of those meetings.

Bailey Benson, Cuatro's grandfather, had been among the group of six cattlemen who founded the association, and Cuatro never missed a conference. He was happy to let everyone know that his granddaddy had been a charter member and that he was carrying on his work.

When Cuatro phoned, he told Boomer that he and Buck Carter wanted him to fly down to Houston to talk. If Boomer were interested, they would get started right away. Boomer was more than interested. This was exactly the kind of project that he had dreamed of since he had left Dungee, Harris, and Schmidt, and he agreed to meet with them the following week.

"We don't want some cookie-cutter plan," Cuatro informed him as soon as the men were settled in the comfortable black leather chairs surrounding the polished mahogany table in the dining room of the Petroleum Club. "Each hotel will be entirely unique. It will reflect the city in which it is built, but we don't want predictable. We're not interested in seeing lariats hanging on the walls and boots on the tables holding flower arrangements. This is Texas, and we want to see Texas in our hotels. We want big, comfortable, and opulent, and we want it built by a Texan. You think this is something you want to take on?"

"I do," said Boomer. "Tell me more."

Cuatro, who was at least twenty years older than either Boomer or Buck, had reached the age where he was old enough to want to tell endless stories about his family but still young enough to remember which ones he had already told. As the waiter deposited enormous sizzling steaks and huge baked potatoes before each of the men, Cuatro smiled contentedly and launched into one of his favorite family histories.

"Did I ever tell you about my great granddaddy Benjamin Boyd Bennett?"

"I don't think so," Boomer replied.

"Well, I'm gonna tell you a little story about him because it relates to why we're here today. It'll help you understand what we're looking for in these hotels."

Buck suppressed a smile. He knew that Cuatro's "little story" had nothing to do with the hotels. Cuatro just wanted an opportunity to talk about the Bennett Ranch and the role his family had played in Texas history.

"My great granddaddy was the youngest of fourteen children. His family had a little dirt farm in Kansas near the Missouri border where they raised a few cows and a big garden to keep the family fed. Ben, bein' the baby and all, came to his parents late in life. His mama was forty when he was born, and she never fully recovered her health after giving birth to him. She died of a stomach ailment when he was fourteen. He lost his dad a year later to an accident when a horse spooked and a hay wagon turned over on him.

"All his brothers and sisters had already left home, and there didn't seem to be any reason to stay on that patch of dirt so Ben left to find his fortune. He had heard that Texas had opportunity and he headed south with just five dollars in his pocket.

"Those were hard years. The War Between the States had ended a few months before Ben got to Texas, and everybody was trying to get their lives back. They had fought Mexico for their independence and finally became an independent republic in 1836. Just nine years later, on the twenty-ninth day of December, they were granted statehood. When the War Between the States broke out, Texas joined the Confederacy, so when the war ended in 1865, there was a lot of rebuilding to be done and a lot of opportunity for a young man who wasn't afraid of work.

""During the next years, Ben learned to ride the range, and he managed to buy a few cattle of his own. When he was twenty-five he took a herd made up of his own cattle and those of several of his friends on a 600 mile trail drive that lasted more than half a year and ended at Marfa. When they reached their destination, Ben separated out his cattle and bought a piece of land at the base of the mountains. That was the beginning of the Bennett Ranch and the Three Crosses brand that would become famous throughout the West.

"Ben Bennett never knew an easy life. He had to deal with drought, rustlers, and disease, but he never gave up. He just kept workin' and trustin' that everything would work out, and he always kept God right in the middle of everything.

"When his son Bailey went off to school, Ben wrote him a letter saying that when he met Nancy Jane Hammond he knew the minute he laid eyes on her that she was the gal for him, but he prayed about it for six months before he asked her to be his wife. He wanted God's blessing on his life, and before he did anything, he worked to make sure that God approved. He told Bailey that if he would keep God in all his decisions, he would find a wife as good as his mother and a life that was a blessing to him and everyone that he came in contact with.

"Ben wasn't just talk. He did a lot of good. He was one of the founders of the First Baptist Church of Marfa, and he set up an endowment so that as long as the ranch was in business the church would receive five percent of the net proceeds and another five percent would go to fund missions to bring Christianity to foreign lands. Those endowments are still in place, and God's work is still being funded by them.

"At Ben's funeral, Luke White, who'd been his friend since he first arrived in Texas, said that the only thing Ben Bennett ever feared was God. Ben once told him that the day he learned the meaning of a healthy fear of the Lord was the day he started down the path to acquiring some wisdom. I guess that was true, but it was also the day that he started acquiring a lot of land and cattle and respect among the other cattlemen.

"After Ben's death Bailey took over the ranch, and he was as good a rancher as my great granddaddy. He married Martha Ann Sheldon whose daddy owned the general store and the livery. They were happy on the ranch, and the second year Mama Benson—that's what we grandchildren called her—gave birth to a girl. A year later she gave birth to a second girl. They were what people in these parts called "Irish twins" because they were only one year apart in age. The first girl Papa Benson named Nancy and the second girl he named Jane. I guess he figured that since he had used up all of his mama's names he didn't need any more children because they never had any others.

"This is the thing that we want you to keep in mind when you're planning the hotels. Texas has always had its share of scalawags and rascals, but it's had more than its share of good God-fearing men, and they're the ones that made this state great.

"My great granddaddy's brand was The Three Crosses. He said that he chose that brand because it tells the story of a man's need for a savior. He wanted everyone who saw it to be reminded that Jesus died on a cross with a thief on either side of Him. Both thieves were dying, and both needed saving, but only one asked to be redeemed. One died mocking the only One who had the power to deliver him, and the other died with the assurance that he was going to be with Him in Heaven that very day.

"People like to say that we are born alone and we die alone. Nothing is further from the truth. Jesus Christ is always right there beside us, just like He was with those two thieves. That's why Ben Bennett wanted the three crosses in his brand—to remind people that even though Jesus is always close by, in the end the decision is theirs."

As Boomer listened to Cuatro's narrative, he wondered whether the old man had any idea how much he had been inspired by it. Cuatro's words gave Boomer the vision he needed, and as he listened he began planning the San Antonio Texas Grand Hotel. He would incorporate the two things for which San Antonio is best known—the Alamo and the River Walk. The liberal use of natural stone, arched doorways, and courtyards with brilliantly-colored flowers and water cascading down ancient-looking stone walls would capture the essence of San Antonio, incorporating elements of both the Alamo and the River Walk.

Boomer knew that when people think of the Alamo, their minds go to the battle fought there between the Texans and the Mexican Army. What few stop to consider is that before it was a battleground, the Alamo was a mission, a house of God. He would incorporate a small room off one of the gardens that would serve as a chapel. It would be in the mission style with stone walls, wooden pews and a dark wooden cross on the end wall—a simple reminder that before the Alamo played a role in the battle for independence, it played a role in the battle for men's souls. Boomer said nothing of his vision for the first project but told Cuatro and Buck that he would have some preliminary drawings for them in a couple of weeks.

Chapter 25

While Boomer was working on the drawings for the San Antonio Texas Grand Hotel, Molly made an unexpected visit. She had phoned a few times, but she had not been home for three years.

Her sudden departure from the family had left a hole in her parents' hearts from which they were unable to recover. It was as if she had died, but there was no closure. If she had been killed in an accident or died of some horrible disease, they would have been able to hold onto the memories of a loving relationship with their sweet beautiful daughter cut short by tragedy.

As it was, each day they were forced to cope with feelings of rejection by one of the two people they loved most in the world. They also had to deal with not knowing where she was or what she was doing. They feared for her safety and for her soul. Boomer battled visions of her being raped or murdered, and Elizabeth fought to control the nightmares that plagued her in which Molly was a little girl and was lost in a dark wood. In her dreams Elizabeth searched and called her name, but she was never able to find her.

That Wednesday morning when Elizabeth answered the phone and heard Molly's voice on the other end, her heart began to pound. It had been months since they had heard from her, and in between phone calls they never knew where she was or what she was doing.

"I'm in town on business," Molly said.

Elizabeth ignored that. She was absolutely certain that Molly had no "business" dealings in the Dallas area. "Are we going to get to see you while you're here?" she asked carefully.

"If you want. Do you want to meet me somewhere?"

"Why don't you come to the house for dinner this evening? We'd love to have you spend the night. Your room is just like you left it."

"I have a lot to do. I can come for dinner, but I can't stay."

"Okay. What time can you be here?"

"Is 6:00 too early?"

"Of course not. You can come right now and spend the day with me. I'd love that."

"I'll see you at 6:00. I can't make it earlier than that."

Elizabeth called Boomer first and then Tracy. Boomer was excited and said that he would be home by 5:30.

Molly had always loved eating outside by the pool, and Elizabeth decided that they would grill steaks and serve dinner alfresco. She spent the rest of the day buying Molly's favorite foods and preparing a poolside celebration that she hoped would remind Molly of all they had shared together as a family and, just maybe, cause her want to be a part of their lives again.

Tracy received the news of Molly's homecoming without enthusiasm. She had seen how much Molly had hurt their parents, and she did not want her around, but she was determined that she would not say anything to upset her mom and dad.

As Tracy entered the kitchen that evening, Elizabeth noticed how beautifully her dark eyes and long chocolate colored hair contrasted with her fair skin. People often commented on how different the girls were in appearance; however, their features and even their facial expressions were very much alike. The main difference was in their coloring. If Molly were the sultry blonde, Tracy was the exotic brunette.

Tracy was wearing a bright red tank and denim shorts. Her feet were bare and her thick hair was pulled into a pony tail that hung to her shoulder blades. She had not bothered to put on shoes when she had changed her clothes after coming home from her afternoon classes at Baylor, and she was enjoying the coolness of the stone floor on her naked feet.

Tracy was finishing her sophomore year and was carrying a 3.85 GPA. She was active in several clubs and seemed to be enjoying the college experience. In addition, she worked for Boomer during her summer vacations. Although her major was elementary education, she liked being at the firm and helped out wherever they needed her.

Tracy and Elizabeth worked well together. Years spent in the kitchen cooking together had taught them to synchronize their chores so that they were able to chat and laugh as they prepared the meal without either asking the other what needed to be done. They would leave the grilling and slicing of the steaks to Boomer, and they would prepare all of the accompaniments for steak fajitas. As they chopped onions, tomatoes, cilantro, and jalapenos, they discussed Tracy's summer plans. Tracy made the guacamole while Elizabeth made the queso. The Fiesta Ware in its greens, yellows and reds that Elizabeth used for poolside dining perfectly complemented the spicy, colorful food.

As 6:00 approached, Elizabeth began to feel nervous. What if Molly did not come? How long should they wait for her before acknowledging that she had stood them up? As Elizabeth turned these thoughts over in her mind, she heard Boomer's car pull into the garage.

"I'll change and get the grill fired up right away," he called as he hurried up the stairs.

Elizabeth looked carefully at Tracy. "You know," she said, "you and Molly are the modern day story of the prodigal son—sort of updated to the prodigal daughter."

Tracy smiled, but did not reply.

"When Molly left, it nearly broke my heart, but you have always been here, and that means everything to me. You are the obedient son who stayed with the father, and like the father and son in the Bible, you and I are very close. We have spent years together sharing our lives and making memories that no one can ever take from us.

"Molly shut Dad and me out of her life a long time ago. We love her as much as we ever did, and we long for the day when she will come back to us, but the time that we could have spent together during these last three years is gone, and every year that she stays away more time is lost. We will never have the kinds of memories with her that we share with you.

"That's why Jesus told the story of the prodigal. People get upset when they read it because they think it's unfair that the prodigal was able to spend his youth going to parties and living in debauchery. He had so much 'fun' while the elder brother just worked on the farm and never had one single celebration with his friends.

"What they miss when they read the story, Honey, is that those parties left the prodigal with absolutely nothing. He was so poor and hungry that even the pods that he fed the pigs began to look good to him. By the time he came to his senses, all of the riches that could have been his through a loving relationship with the father were lost. He came home and was welcomed with open arms, but all of those wasted years were just that—wasted. He was no longer a part of anything that had been built in his absence.

"Someday soon you will marry and have a home of your own, but even after you leave this house, everything that we have shared together will continue to impact our lives. I want to thank you for giving me the gift of your friendship."

Elizabeth was interrupted by the sound of the doorbell. Checking her watch, she saw that it was five minutes before 6:00. One thing had not changed; Molly was still punctual.

Chapter 26

$\mathcal{A}$t first glance, it appeared that Molly had not changed. When one looked closer, however, it was apparent that the last three years had been hard on her. Her heavy makeup made her appear older than her twenty-two years. She was wearing so much black eyeliner and dark eye shadow that it was nearly impossible to tell the color of her eyes. Normally when Molly sat next to the pool her eyes were a perfect match for the deep blue of the water. Now, however, the dark makeup prevented them from reflecting the light so that their color seemed to disappear.

Molly was still thin, but it was apparent that she had not been exercising. Her body was soft, and her cheap knit shorts showed the beginnings of a slight pot belly. Her skin and hair looked as if they had been scorched by a hot wind. She was still beautiful, but the freshness and sparkle were gone.

As Molly wrapped one of the freshly made flour tortillas around several slices of perfectly cooked steak and piled on guacamole, she began talking. The more she talked, the faster her words came. It was as if she were afraid that someone else would say something or ask her a question. She said that she was working for a firm in Los Angeles that designed sets for television and movies.

"It's different from what you do," she said looking at Boomer. "Sets have to be bigger than life. They have to create an impact. Not boring stuff like the designs for offices."

Elizabeth saw Boomer's eyes flash, but he answered with perfect control, "What's the name of the firm you work for?"

"It's new; it's going through a name change, and they're not sure what name they're going to settle on."

"What movies have they worked on?"

"Oh, a whole bunch. Stuff with Tom Cruise and Johnny Depp. Big movies."

"And television shows?"

"Uh, we're doing the sets for some pilots that will come out next season. One's about a lawyer with a great office— that kind of stuff. Anyway, I've got the best job in LA. I love design, and I think I will probably have an Emmy or an Oscar in a few years."

"All of this without a degree?" Boomer asked.

"I'm going to finish school. I'm just going to get my degree in set design instead of that boring design for commercial projects."

Molly looked at Tracy, "What are you going to do when you finish school?"

"I'm getting my degree in elementary education. I'll teach after I graduate."

"Pleeeeeeeeeease," Molly wrinkled her nose, "I wouldn't be stuck in a classroom with a bunch of brats for anything.

You need to get out of here and start doing something that has a future!"

"I'm thinking about starting my own television game show," Tracy retorted. "I'm going to call it *First Liar doesn't have a Chance*. You can be my first guest."

Molly gulped and finished her fajita in silence. By that time Elizabeth had turned the conversation to less toxic topics, and for the remainder of the evening Molly was much more subdued. As the evening wore on, Molly began to relax, and it was apparent to her parents that she was enjoying herself.

She stayed until after midnight, and when she was ready to leave Elizabeth wrapped her in her arms and held her for a long time. "I want your e-mail address and your cell phone number," she said as she released Molly from her grasp. "I don't have any way to get in touch with you."

"Sure," Molly replied.

After she had written down the information, Elizabeth said, "Don't stay away so long. I love you, and I miss you. This is your home. You are always welcome here."

"Okay," Molly replied, and she turned and walked out the door.

Chapter 27

*J*ames stood just outside the secured area of the San Antonio airport holding a sign that read, "Anderson." Billy Ferguson was supposed to meet the plane, but at the last minute there had been an accident at one of the construction sites. As he had headed out the door he had told James to pick up some guy from Dallas who was hiring Ferguson Building Corp. to build a hotel.

James did not know how he was supposed to recognize this guy, but Billy had told him that his name was something or other Anderson so James made a little cardboard sign like the ones he had seen other uncomfortable-looking young people holding when they were forced to pick up passengers they did not know. James was rather artistic and had used a black felt marker to produce a very satisfactory sign. Now as he stood in his paint-splattered jeans and tennis shoes holding the sign so that the passengers could see it as they passed through the gate, he felt ridiculous.

A tall muscular guy with thick dark hair and even darker eyes was walking toward the gate. He was wearing an expensive suit, a dress shirt with gold cufflinks, and cowboy boots. "I hope that's not him," James thought.

As the man approached, he caught sight of the sign and smiled broadly. Extending his hand, he said, "I'm Boomer Anderson!"

James returned the smile, but he was very nervous. This was one of those rich guys. He would probably think James was a loser. Suddenly, James was very aware of his own shabby attire.

"Billy Ferguson sent me to pick you up because we had an accident at one of the job sites, and he had to go over there. He said to apologize to you for not being here himself."

"No problem. Thanks for coming. I could have taken a cab."

Boomer's voice was deep and loud—the kind that attracts everyone's attention. "No wonder they call him Boomer," James thought.

James tried to carry Boomer's bag, but he told him that he would carry it himself. When they arrived at the company truck in the parking lot, Boomer climbed into the cab, and looking at James, he asked, "You had lunch yet?"

"No, Sir."

"Me either, and I'm starved. Go through the drive thru at McDonalds—my treat."

James drove to Ferguson Building Corp. while they ate their Big Macs and fries. Boomer asked James about himself and then launched into a lengthy story about how he had met Billy.

"I met Billy Ferguson the first time I attended a meeting of the Texas Christian Ranchers Association," Boomer said. "He and I just clicked. You know how sometimes you meet someone, and it's like you've known them all your life? Well, that's how it was with Billy and me. Even though he's older, we had a lot in common. Billy had been in the association for a while, and he took me under his wing and introduced me around. After that we kept in touch, and whenever I need to partner with a builder in San Antonio, Billy's my go-to man."

Boomer talked during most of the drive, and when he finally paused, James thought that he should say something, but he could not think of anything that would not sound dumb, so he blurted out, "Those are great boots!"

"Thanks," Boomer replied. "There's nothing like a good pair of boots. I have a boot maker in Dallas who makes them for me, and I can tell you that once you get used to wearing boots, you can't wear anything else.

"Alvarez makes all the boots for Chuck Norris and Tim McGraw and Trace Atkins. You need to get yourself a pair. A good pair of boots lasts for years, so you can consider them an investment."

"I'll be able to afford a pair of those the same day the Martians invade Manhattan."

Boomer threw his head back and laughed loudly."You never know. God may have some boots for you sooner than you think."

By the time James and Boomer arrived at the office Billy had returned. James quickly slipped away and returned to his painting. For the rest of the afternoon as he worked James tried to imagine what it would be like to be Boomer

Anderson. He was old—at least fifty—but he was handsome, and he was rich. He probably had all sorts of women after him.

James wanted to dislike Boomer, and he certainly felt a twinge of jealousy when he thought about the way Boomer lived, but Boomer had been so nice to him that he could not really dislike him. He was glad, though, that he would not see him again. James was certain that, no matter how friendly Boomer Anderson seemed, he really thought that he was a loser.

To James' horror, when he entered the office-trailer at the job site that evening to punch his time card, Billy announced that James was going to be responsible for driving Boomer while he was in San Antonio. "It's just for a few days, and I'll get Boyd to fill in for you here. You just make yourself available to take Mr. Anderson wherever he wants to go."

James felt his heart sink. "Yes, sir. I'll see you in the morning." Then turning toward Boomer, he said, "Good night, Mr. Anderson."

"Pick me up tomorrow morning at seven. I'll meet you in the hotel coffee shop," Boomer replied.

James spent the next three days driving Boomer to construction sites and meetings. Boomer was so pleasant that after the first day James relaxed a little. For such a fit man Boomer ate a lot, and he always paid for James' meals. By the third day James was sorry that his assignment was coming to an end.

On Friday evening when James dropped Boomer off at his hotel, Boomer announced that his wife had driven up from Dallas to spend the weekend before they drove home on Monday. As Boomer climbed out of the truck, a beautiful blonde woman walked out the door of the hotel and spotted them.

"Lizzie!" Boomer shouted. "Come over here and meet James. He's been my driver all week."

Elizabeth smiled and shook hands with James. "Thanks for taking care of him," she said.

"No problem. You all have a good weekend," James said.

As he drove away he thought that Boomer Anderson was probably the luckiest man he had ever met.

Six weeks later Billy told James to come to his office. On the desk was a large box addressed to James. Inside was the most beautiful pair of boots James had ever seen. On top was a card that read, "The Martians have landed." It was signed, "Boomer Anderson."

James slipped the boots on and was amazed to discover that they fit perfectly. Puzzled he looked at Billy, "How did he know my size?"

"You gotta watch us old guys," Billy laughed. "We're sneaky, and when we have keys to your apartment, it's not too hard to get in and find your extra pair of shoes."

From that day forward whenever James was not on the construction site, those boots were on his feet.

Chapter 28

$\mathcal{B}$y the time James met Boomer he had been involved in CR for nearly three years.

When James had finished all but his final three weeks of CR, he stayed one night to talk to Tony about what he should do after he completed the program.

"I'm not ready to be on my own," James had confessed. "Here I get the strength to make it through the week. I'm afraid that when it ends, I'll start using again. It's not even that I'm really all that tempted. I just don't know how to get along without the group."

"Let me tell you about myself," Tony replied.

"I came to celebrate recovery because my wife took my kids and left me, and I knew that unless I made some big time changes she wasn't ever going to come back. I never had an affair, and I didn't use drugs. We had been married fifteen years, and I had never hit her. I drank very little, and I had a good-paying job as the CFO for Mercy Hospital. I loved Shelly, and I loved my kids, but I was unhappy.

"I grew up lower middle-class. My dad grew up poor, and even though he worked hard and gave us a normal life, he always worried about money. He taught his kids to work and to save, and to never waste anything. He was never physically abusive, but he had a temper, and he and my mom engaged in frequent screaming matches. He yelled at us kids a lot too. He was always afraid that something terrible would happen, and we would all end up on the street. Every time we bought anything that he considered frivolous, even though we bought it with money we earned ourselves, he flew into a rage.

"My mom learned to ignore him, and I think that after a while she learned to hate him. She never said anything disrespectful about him to us kids, but when he died, she never shed a tear. While he was alive, Mom acted as a buffer between him and the kids. She kept us out of his way as much as she could, and she kept a lot of things hidden from him. 'Don't tell Dad,' became the most common phrase in our house. It wasn't that she was keeping anything important from him; she just didn't want to deal with his temper when we did something that made him mad. And she knew that just about everything that we did would get us into trouble with him.

"When I married, I didn't know how to be a husband or a father. I had been afraid for as long as I could remember, but I thought that financial success would take away that fear. I achieved my goals of the six-figure income, a nice house, and two new cars, but I was never able to shake the fear. It was like a cold lump that sat in my stomach and tugged at my heart.

"When I realized that all my hard work had not made me feel safe, I became angry, and with each passing day the anger grew hotter. I was constantly yelling at my wife and kids, and whenever I got started, the anger seemed to swell inside of me. I could actually feel it burning in my chest like a fire, and I would rave for hours.

"On the Friday after school let out for the summer I came home to an empty house. Shelly had taken the kids and gone to her parents' home in Tulsa. She had left a note on the kitchen counter, 'I can't live like this anymore. The kids and I are at my mom and dad's. Don't call or try to see us. I'm filing for divorce.'

"I felt like someone had just punched me in the stomach, but rather than trying to figure out what to do to get my family back, I flew into a rage. The only thing Shelly and the kids had taken with them was their clothes, and I walked through the house screaming and throwing things. I kicked the furniture and broke a few dishes, but my anger only intensified.

"I had a full bottle of bourbon and some beer in the house, and after I finished my tantrum, I started drinking. I spent the whole weekend sitting in my chair in a drunken stupor. On Monday I went back to work at the hospital, but every evening I drank non-stop. The next few months are a blur. I just drank and vented to the empty rooms.

"By the middle of October I knew that I had to get sobered up; my work was suffering, and I knew that if I didn't shape up I would get fired, so I cut back on my drinking and started eating better. One day I was buying some groceries, and I ran into one of the ambulance drivers that I knew from the hospital. He asked if I had been sick, and that was the first time I realized how much of a toll my four-month binge had taken on me. I had lost weight, my hair was a mess, and my clothes looked as if I had slept in them.

"He invited me to have coffee with him, and I was so lonely that I accepted. We went to a Denny's across the street, and over coffee I told him about Shelly leaving me. It was Wednesday, and he invited me to go to church with him that evening. Church was the last place I wanted to be, but Greg was the only person with whom I had talked for weeks, and I felt that I couldn't face going back to that empty house.

"Greg was an older guy who had lost his wife to cancer a year earlier, and his kids, who had families of their own, had moved away. His schedule was as flexible as mine, and he insisted that we have a burger and then head over to the church. Well, as it turned out, this was the church that he brought me to.

"I had never gone to church much. My mother was a devout Catholic, but Dad did not believe in going to church. Shelly was a Baptist, and she and the kids attended church fairly regularly, but she never encouraged me to go with her. Looking back, I think she was glad to get away from me for a couple of hours on Sunday.

"Anyway, I only went to church that Wednesday because I was so lonely that I thought I just couldn't face another evening alone; I certainly never expected to go back, but Greg introduced me to several of the men, and everyone was so friendly that I returned on Sunday morning. That was when I picked up a bulletin that told about Celebrate Recovery. I realized that I had a lot of 'hurts, habits, and hang-ups' that I needed to deal with, and when Greg suggested that I join one of the groups, I agreed.

"I felt really comfortable in the group. I was afraid that I would find myself in with a bunch of child molesters and crazed addicts who would try to follow me home and kill me for the money in my wallet, but I soon discovered that my group consisted of six other men who were pretty much like me. Our problems were different, but our situations were the same. Our habits and hang-ups had brought us to a place where we were on the brink of losing everything that was important to us, and we wanted to turn our lives around.

"When I was about half-way through the program, I was at home one night reading my Bible when I suddenly realized that Celebrate Recovery wasn't teaching me to deal with my anger; it was teaching me how to be a Christian. I began crying and thanking God for sending Greg to me and...."

James interrupted, "Say that again!"

"I began crying and...."

"No, not that. The part about what CR was teaching you."

"CR wasn't teaching me how to deal with my anger; it was teaching me how to be a Christian."

"That's it! I'm learning how to be a Christian, and I'm not ready to be on my own yet!" James exclaimed.

"Well, Jimbo, I hate to be the one to tell you this, but you'll never be ready to be on your own. The Bible says that Christians should not neglect meeting together. That's the only way that we can stay on a steady course. We share our faith with each other and help one another through the rough spots. When we see a Christian brother getting on the wrong track, we're there to pull him back. You'll never get past needing the fellowship of other Christians, and if you think about it, you probably wouldn't want to. The alternative is to fellowship with non-Christians, and we both know where that leads."

"Can I go through CR a second time?"

"Sure, you can go through it as many times as you feel like it."

James did go through CR a second time, but then Tony suggested that he go to California and train to be a CR leader. Billy Ferguson gave James the time off he needed to take the leadership training and insisted on keeping him on the payroll while he was gone.

James returned to San Antonio ready to lead a group, and when the next sessions opened, he became a CR leader. It was the happiest he had ever been, and every week his passion for CR increased until he knew that he wanted to spend the rest of his life helping men break free from their personal demons and give their lives to Jesus.

Meeting Boomer had presented James with a new dilemma. He had become accustomed to taking on the leadership role. The men he worked with were always asking him for advice and counsel. He had felt strong and wise as he had worked with those men, but now he had met someone who would never think of asking him for advice. For the first time in a long time James felt vulnerable.

Boomer had treated him well. James knew that any negative feelings were strictly on his side, but he was glad that Boomer had returned to Dallas. When he was with Boomer, he was aware that he had fallen short; he would never be rich and important, and he didn't want people around him who made him feel that he should aspire to better things in his own life.

Chapter 29

In December of 2017 Tracy completed the first semester of her senior year. She was glad for the Christmas break and glad that in January she would begin her final semester. She had enjoyed college, but she was tired of being in school and looking forward to helping Boomer out at the firm during the break.

Gloria, his long-time receptionist, had asked for the week before Christmas off so that she could go to Vermont to spend the holiday with her parents who were in their eighties. Tracy was only too glad to fill in for her.

The offices were beautifully decorated for the holidays in deep cranberry reds, forest greens, gold and silver. Tracy was reminded of all the times she had come to visit her dad at those offices during her school breaks when she was a little girl. They had seemed to her like a magical winter wonderland, and her opinion had not changed. She felt her spirits rise every time she walked through the door.

The employee lunch room was piled high with all sorts of holiday treats. Cookies, candies, nuts, crackers, and cheese balls covered the counter top. Christmas music played softly throughout the offices. Within those walls Tracy felt completely content, and she smiled with a child's delight as she popped one of the Godiva chocolates that she had placed on her desk into her mouth.

As soon as she had done it, she realized that the piece was far too big for one bite. She covered her mouth with her hand and chewed furiously, trying to swallow part of it before anyone saw her. Before she succeeded, however, the door opened and the most handsome man she had ever seen walked into the reception area. Horrified, Tracy turned her back and swallowed the chocolate mass in one gulp. Wiping her mouth with her bare hand, she turned back to face the young man standing in front of her desk.

His blue eyes sparkled, and the amused look on his face signaled that she had not been successful in hiding her indiscretion. She knew that if she smiled her teeth would be full of chocolate so she kept her face very serious and asked, "May I help you?"

"My name is Charles Davenport. I have an appointment with Bradley Anderson."

"One moment please," Tracy said as she rose from her chair and disappeared down the hall. She ran straight to the bathroom, rinsed her mouth profusely, checked her teeth in the mirror, applied new lipstick, and returned to the reception area. She was now so embarrassed that she couldn't smile.

"Mr. Anderson will see you now. Down the hall; last door to your right."

Charles Martin Davenport III was twenty-six years old and had worked for a prestigious architectural firm in Boston since earning his degree. He had enjoyed the work, but he was a Texas boy and wanted to return to his home state. Boomer had already checked him out. He had reviewed his grade transcripts and discovered that he was an A student and had been active in several clubs in college. His references were impeccable; from all indications Charles Martin Davenport III was a hard-working, intelligent young man who had stayed out of trouble and gained the respect of those who knew him.

Boomer knew his father, and when Charles Davenport II had heard that he was looking for an architect to bring into the firm, he had called Boomer himself to set up the interview. Boomer had agreed because of their relationship, but he was determined that if the young Charles Davenport were found lacking he would not be given a job. Now, as he sat across the desk from the young man, Boomer was far more impressed than he had imagined he would be.

"What shall we call you?" Boomer asked. "Charles? Charlie?"

"My Grandpa is Charlie, and my Dad goes by Chuck. When I was a kid, my mom called me Charles, but with all three of us having the same name it got pretty confusing. When I was sixteen, I decided to use my middle name, and I asked everyone to call me Marty."

"I'm wondering why you chose architecture. Since your family has always been in the oil business, it seems like an unlikely choice."

"Ever since I can remember I've loved buildings. When I was still in elementary school my mom used to take my sisters and me to various museums. Everyone else looked at the art, and I looked at the architecture. To me the real art was the beautiful old buildings with their carved woodwork and intricate detail."

"When I was a little older, I would walk around our neighborhood looking at the houses and imagine how I would change certain details to make them even better. I'm afraid that I still do that. I never enter a building without imagining how I would redesign it if given the chance."

Boomer listened as Marty talked on and on about his love of architectural design. Although he did not say so, he understood exactly how Marty felt. He had known while he was still in middle school that he wanted to design buildings, but he had not found many people who shared his love of architecture. Marty was exactly the kind of person he wanted to bring into the firm.

"When will you be available?" Boomer asked.

"I need to give my employer thirty days notice. Their policy is to cut anyone loose immediately once they give notice. I can't imagine that they would want me to stay on for thirty days, but I would feel obligated to do so if that's what they wanted."

"Do you feel that Bradley Anderson and Associates would be a good fit for you?"

"Yes, I do. I checked out your website and also found out quite a lot about the firm from various other sources. Your projects are exactly the kind that I love working on."

"Good," Boomer extended his hand. "Tender your resignation, and let me know when you can start. Since you're going to be joining us, why don't you come to the employee Christmas party this Saturday. That way you can meet everyone."

"I'd love to."

"You can get all the particulars from Tracy at the front desk."

When Marty reached the reception area, he told Tracy that he had been hired and that Mr. Anderson had invited him to the Christmas party on Saturday.

She wrote the time and the name and address of the restaurant on a piece of note paper and handed it to him. Turning the note over in his hand, Marty asked, "Are you going to be there?"

"Of course, I never miss a Christmas party." Tracy was still a little embarrassed, but Marty was so disarming that she smiled in spite of herself.

"Okay then, I'll see you Saturday," and with that he turned and walked out the door.

Chapter 30

The party was held in a large private dining room of an upscale restaurant that had been the site of Bradley Anderson and Associates' Christmas party for the past ten years. It was built in the Old World style with a huge stone fireplace dominating one wall and massive chandeliers hanging from the ceiling. As Tracy looked around the room, she thought that being there was like stepping back in time to a Christmas in some far away magical land.

Nearly all of the female guests had worn their most festive holiday attire; even Elizabeth was dressed in sapphire silk with matching sapphire and diamond jewelry. Tracy, however, had chosen a simple black dress, and her only jewelry was a pair of pearl and diamond earrings with a matching ring. Her hair cascaded down her back in soft curls, and her skin glowed like ivory in the candlelight.

Tracy was talking with a group of employees when she saw Marty come through the door. Her first impulse was to rush over to greet him, but she stayed where she was and acknowledged him with a smile. Turning back to the other employees, Tracy gave them her attention.

Within minutes she felt Elizabeth's hand on her arm. "Tracy, there's someone Dad wants you to meet."

As she moved across the room, Tracy felt as if she were walking on air. "This is the best Christmas of my life," she thought.

As Tracy and Elizabeth neared, Boomer turned toward them. "Didn't you meet my daughter the other day?" Boomer asked.

Tracy was watching Marty carefully. Although he tried hard not to react to those words, she saw that the news had startled him.

"Yes sir, she helped me out at the front desk."

Tracy smiled brightly. She was now the one with the advantage, and she could not help enjoying seeing Marty squirm a little.

"Well," Boomer continued, "Tracy's going to introduce you around. Make sure he meets everybody, Honey."

"I will, Dad."

Before the day of his interview Marty had never met anyone whom he had seriously considered marrying, but before he had left the offices of Bradley Anderson and Associates that day, he knew that he was going to marry Tracy. While his new boss would probably have no objection to having Marty marry his receptionist, he might well object to having him marry his daughter. Marty was not prepared for this additional challenge, and he was not sure how he would be able make this marriage happen, but he was determined that it would happen.

As soon as Marty and Tracy walked away, Boomer pulled Elizabeth closer and whispered, "That boy doesn't know it yet, but he's gonna be my son-in-law."

"What? You think he's going to marry Tracy?"

"I know he is. I started praying for her husband right after she started at Baylor, and the minute I laid eyes on him I knew he was the one. Don't get me wrong; I would have hired him anyway, but I'm glad that when I eventually make him a partner he'll already be part of the family."

"Tracy might have something to say about this," Elizabeth responded.

"As long as that something is 'yes' we'll be just fine," Boomer said grinning from ear to ear.

Chapter 31

*I*t was a warm afternoon in April. Elizabeth was sitting at her desk which was positioned in the bay window of the master bedroom suite. Boomer had designed it so that the soft green granite top was custom fit into the space. Whenever she sat at the desk, Elizabeth had a bird's eye view of her "white garden." The numerous plants were beginning to bloom, and the contrast of the gorgeous creamy flowers against the greenery was breathtaking.

Marty had returned to Dallas and begun work on January 15, and from the day he arrived back in town he and Tracy had been inseparable. The third week in February Tracy had informed her parents that Marty wanted to talk to them, and they had set up an appointment for him to come to the house the following Saturday afternoon.

It was cold and rainy that day, and a fire roared in the fireplace of the library. Boomer sat in his grandfather's chair across from Elizabeth and Marty who were seated on the tobacco-colored leather couch. Boomer and Elizabeth sipped the freshly brewed coffee, but Marty left his steaming mug untouched. It was clear that he was nervous—more so than he had been when he had interviewed for his job.

"I love Tracy," he began. "I have asked her to marry me, and I would like for you to give us your blessing."

"You have my blessing," Elizabeth responded. She was well aware of how much Tracy loved Marty, and she had observed that he loved her too. Normally, she would have been opposed to a couple who had known each other for only a little more than four weeks becoming engaged, but she knew that Marty was a Christian and that he was very serious about his feelings for Tracy. His parents were long-time Christians who had raised him well. Elizabeth was certain that this marriage was ordained by God.

"Not so fast!" Boomer said without smiling. "First I have a question for you!" What seemed like a long pause followed before he continued, "What took you so long?"

Marty looked immensely relieved, and Boomer burst out laughing.

Afterwards, Boomer commented to Elizabeth that he was impressed that Marty had asked for their permission to marry Tracy.

"He didn't ask for our permission; he asked for our blessing," she replied. "I listened very carefully to everything Marty said. He let us know that he was going to marry Tracy no matter what we thought, but he also wanted us to know that he would prefer that we give them our blessing."

"Good for him!" Boomer said. "A man should go after what he wants."

Now, as Elizabeth sat staring out the window, she thought about Molly. She had spent the last hour addressing invitations for Tracy's wedding, and she could not help contrasting her girls' lives. Tracy was preparing to marry her dream man in the perfect wedding. Her future in-laws were well-respected members of the community who were welcoming her into their family with open arms. Everything in Tracy's life was just about perfect.

Elizabeth understood that Molly's problems were the result of her own poor choices, but that knowledge did not make it easier for her to deal with the mess that Molly had made of her life. "If Molly would get her life straightened out," Elizabeth thought, "this would be the happiest time of my life." For a long time she continued to stare out the window as hot tears coursed down her cheeks and dropped onto the desk.

Elizabeth spent the next hour praying for Molly. She prayed for Molly every day, but sometimes she felt a special need to increase those prayers. She was still sitting at her desk when Tracy came home from school.

When Tracy entered the room, she asked, "What's the matter, Mom?"

"I was just thinking about Molly. I wish that she had made better choices. I wonder whether I will ever be helping her plan her wedding."

Elizabeth wiped her eyes and forced a smile, "Are you going to invite her to the wedding?"

"I talked to Marty about it, and he said that I absolutely should invite her. He said that family is important and that no matter what she's done, she's still part of our family. I know all of that's true, but I also know Molly. I don't mind having her there, but I'm afraid that she will do something to embarrass all of us. Your friends and his parents' friends will be attending, and I'm afraid that she'll pull one of her stunts."

"It's your wedding, and it's up to you. Let me know what you decide, and that's what we'll do."

"I don't need to think about it any more," Tracy replied. "Invite her."

Elizabeth called Molly the next morning when she was alone in the house. Molly was in a talkative mood and rattled on for twenty minutes before Elizabeth extended the invitation.

"We're sending you a printed invitation," Elizabeth said, "but I wanted to talk to you too. I hope that you will come."

"When is it?"

"June 3rd at our church."

"I guess."

"June 3rd is on a Saturday, so I was thinking that if you could come in on Wednesday we could go shopping for your dress and you could go with Tracy and me on Saturday morning to have our hair and make-up done. I'll go ahead and set up your appointment too."

"You don't think I have anything to wear?" Molly sounded testy.

"Molly, I hardly ever get to see you. I want to do something special for you. I thought we could go over to Neiman Marcus and you could pick out something you like. It will be fun to have a shopping day—just the two of us."

Elizabeth heard Molly sigh on the other end of the line. "Oh, I guess."

"You'll be here for sure on May 31?"

"I said I would."

"Okay, sweetie. I'll be talking to you before then."

Chapter 32

The guests had taken their seats and Elizabeth and Marty's parents had been seated in the appropriate pews. As Elizabeth waited for the Wedding March to begin, a flood of emotions washed over her. Molly was seated several rows behind her with Pam Greely and two other women from the office. Elizabeth knew that Molly was not happy about being seated with them, but she also knew that Pam would have a settling effect on her. Molly had known Pam for years, and she knew that Pam would report any inappropriate conduct to Boomer.

Molly looked gorgeous. She and Elizabeth had chosen a turquoise silk dress that brought out the blue of her eyes. Her hair and makeup had been done to perfection by the stylists at The Golden Door Salon and Spa. No one would believe that she had been living anything except the life of a pampered young woman who did not have a care in the world. Still, Elizabeth knew the truth, and her heart ached as she waited for Tracy's entrance.

Her thoughts were interrupted by the first strains of the Wedding March. Everyone stood and turned to view the bride as she made her way down the isle. Elizabeth had been with Tracy during every phase of the planning of the wedding, but even though she had seen her in her gown during fittings and had been with her in the bride's room just prior to the ceremony, she was unprepared for the sight of her on Boomer's arm as she glided down the aisle. She was so beautiful that she seemed unreal. It was not just her physical beauty; she possessed a radiance and purity that literally shone out from her like an internal light. Her snowy gown and delicate veil added to the fairy princess quality.

As Boomer placed Tracy's hand in Marty's, Elizabeth looked at the groom. She had never seen any groom look that happy—not even Boomer at their wedding. The perfection of the church, the radiance of the bride and groom, and the beauty of the ceremony only added to Elizabeth' sadness. She prayed silently that God would help Molly to remember what it had been like to have a relationship with Him. She prayed that Molly would come back to the truth and that she would become the woman that God had created her to be. Then she prayed that, when the time was right, God would send Molly a Christian husband who would love her the way Christ loves the Church and that Molly would love him in return. Even as she prayed, however, she doubted that Molly would ever return to Christ, and she was nearly certain that she would not marry a Christian.

Molly was subdued during the reception, but Elizabeth detected a nervous tension in her that led her to believe that Molly would make her escape as soon as possible. Elizabeth had hoped that with Tracy leaving for Italy the next day, Molly would be open to the idea of spending a few days with Boomer and her. She had even gone so far as to make plans for the three of them to do some of the things Molly had enjoyed when she was living at home.

The following morning Molly entered the kitchen as Elizabeth was putting on the coffee. "What would you like for breakfast, Sweetheart?" Elizabeth asked.

"I don't have time for breakfast. My plane leaves at 11:00, and I need to be at the airport early."

Elizabeth was puzzled. She had purchased Molly's ticket and made the reservations herself. "Your return's not until Thursday," she responded.

"I changed my ticket. I have to get back."

"Why did you do that? Dad and I want to spend some time with you."

"I'm busy. I only came to make you happy. Now I need to go."

"Okay, I'll drive you to the airport."

Chapter 33

$\mathcal{M}$olly's flight landed at LAX at 1:30 Sunday afternoon. She was angrier than she had been for a long time. She was sick and tired of hearing how perfect Tracy was and what a wonderful guy she had married. She knew what her parents were doing; they were throwing Tracy in her face to make her feel guilty.

When Molly was a child, Elizabeth had once told her that nine times out of ten when people feel guilty it's because they are. That statement had made Molly uncomfortable at the time, and she had never forgotten it. Now, as she thought about it, she was filled with rage.

"Well, it's not going to work!" she thought as she made her way to the baggage claim. "The only thing I'm guilty of is trying to live my own life out from under their control. I'm not their prisoner, and they're not going to tell me what to do. I hate Tracy, and I hate that stupid dumb-looking kiss-up she married. He's the biggest geek I ever saw. I wouldn't be in Tracy's shoes for anything!"

Actually, neither Elizabeth nor Boomer had said much about Tracy to Molly, and their silence concerning her was intentional. They did not want Molly to feel that they were comparing her life to Tracy's.

The only thing Boomer had said about Marty was that he was a smart guy and seemed to love Tracy. Although Molly knew that Marty worked for him, Boomer did not discuss Marty's position with Bradley Anderson Associates because he thought it would dredge up memories of all the trouble that Molly had caused by pretending that she wanted to be part of the firm.

When Molly had asked Elizabeth what she thought about Marty, Elizabeth had answered that he was a Christian and that she believed that he would be a good husband to Tracy.

"But he's so ugly!" Molly had exclaimed.

Elizabeth had been taken aback by her remark. Of all the things that anyone might say to describe Marty, "ugly" would be at the very bottom of the list. In fact, all of her friends had remarked about what a "gorgeous" couple Tracy and Marty made.

"You think so?" Elizabeth had replied.

"I think he's hideous!" Molly had responded.

Elizabeth had then turned the conversation to another subject.

Molly spotted her bag on the carrousel and stepped forward to snatch it as it passed. Inside that canvas bag was the turquoise silk Neiman Marcus dress. "What a joke!" she fumed silently. "I might as well be a nun if I'm going to dress like that!"

Molly had planned to leave the dress hanging in the closet of her parents' house, but then she realized that a fifteen hundred dollar designer dress would easily sell on e-bay for at least a hundred dollars. Some old woman would probably buy it the first day. She would keep the shoes. They were hot, and she could wear them clubbing.

Molly threw her bag into the backseat of her car and tore out of the airport parking lot. She lit a cigarette and turned her radio up to a deafening level. She felt a little better as she headed toward her apartment. Miguel was tending bar at Oscaritos tonight, but she had the night off; she would go out and see if she could hook up with someone interesting.

When she reached her apartment, the door was locked although Miguel's car was in its parking space. As she turned her key and pushed the door open, she was greeted with the odor of stale beer, sweat, and decaying food. The remnants of partially eaten burgers, onions, and pizza in their carry-out containers were piled on the table, but it was the odor of spoiled fish that nearly made Molly gag. Miguel had thrown his empty sardine cans into the trash again. The heat and lack of ventilation had turned the air inside the apartment into a nauseating stew of odors that made Molly reel.

Before Molly had a chance to react to the stench, however, her eyes fell on various items of women's clothing scattered around the living room: a pink bra, a green thong, a worn denim mini skirt, and a tee shirt with huge red lips made from sequins and a caption that read, "kiss me".

Instantly, the rage that had subsided during Molly's drive to the apartment returned full force. She dropped her bag on the floor and marched into the bedroom. Miguel was sprawled across the bed with his mouth open snoring loudly. Veronica, a Cocktail at Oscaritos, was lying beside him with her long hair hanging off the bed. Molly walked directly to

Veronica and taking her hair in both hands gave a mighty tug that landed the small woman onto the floor.

Next, she grabbed Miguel by the hair and slapped his face repeatedly. It took a few seconds for him to respond, but he was quickly on his feet pushing Molly toward the wall. She felt his fist come down hard on her face, and she quickly raised her arms to ward off further blows.

Molly could hear Veronica and Miguel jabbering to each other in Spanish, most of which she did not understand, and then the sound of someone running from the room and the front door slamming.

Miguel continued to punch Molly with his fist until he knocked her to the floor. Then he kicked her repeatedly with his bare feet until he sprained his toe and collapsed on the bed holding his foot and rubbing the damaged toe.

Molly lay on the floor in a heap. She was badly bruised, and one rib was cracked, but she was not seriously hurt. Neither she nor Miguel spoke, and she did not get up from the floor until he had pulled on his jeans and tee shirt and left the apartment.

As Molly allowed the water in the shower to run over her head and body, she regretted having provoked Miguel. She had been ordered to complete 120 hours of community service by Judge Warren Ottis when she had stood before him in his courtroom after becoming involved in an incident at the club where she worked. One of the other Cocktails had accused her of assault, and since it was not clear to the judge which girl had landed the first blow, he had sentenced them both to community service. Molly still had 60 hours to complete, and she had to report to the county hospital at 8:00 A.M. Monday morning to make beds and deliver meals to the patients. She knew that there would be questions about the swelling and bruises, and she did not look forward to trying to answer them.

The first person Molly saw when the elevator door opened and she stepped out onto the fourth floor of the hospital was Cathy Reynolds. Cathy, who was only three years away from retirement, was the head nurse. Years of managing the nursing staff and dealing with difficult patients had taken away any propensity for the polite small talk that one expects to encounter in a well-placed professional.

As Molly approached, Cathy narrowed her small blue eyes and frowned. Although her shift had begun only two hours earlier, she already looked tired and frazzled. Strands of gray-streaked blonde hair had escaped from her stubby pony tail and hung limply at the sides of her face, and her pink skin was more florid than usual due to the haste with which she was walking down the hallway.

"What happened to you?" she asked as she stopped and planted her feet firmly in the middle of the hall.

"I fell," Molly replied as she attempted to walk past her.

Cathy's hand shot out and caught Molly's arm. "Uh, huh, when I was married, I fell down the stairs all the time—every time my ex got ticked off about something. Funny thing is, I've been divorced for ten years now, and I haven't fallen since. You need to kick that bum out. You'll be surprised how much your balance will improve."

Molly was furious, but she could not afford to antagonize Cathy so she did not reply.

When it was time for her break, Molly poured herself a cup of coffee and went into the nurses' lounge. She was sore and stiff and her rib throbbed. Her eye was black and her lip was split. She looked and felt awful.

As she sipped the hot brew, she sank back into the chair and allowed herself to relax. Just as she had gotten fairly comfortable, the door opened and Cathy entered.

"I want to talk to you," Cathy announced.

"Good grief!" Molly thought, but she tried to force a smile. "Okay."

"I've been watching you since you started here. You're a good worker. I realize that making beds and delivering meal trays isn't the most interesting job on the ward, but you have a good bedside manner. The patients like you, and when you're not here they ask for you. Have you ever thought about going into nursing?"

Molly shrugged, "Not really."

"Well, think about it. There aren't many jobs where you know at the end of the day that you've really helped people. On a good day, you might even save someone's life."

"Yeah, I will," Molly lied. She then laid her head back and closed her eyes. When she opened them five minutes later, Cathy was gone.

Chapter 34

James sat alone praying in one of the deserted CR rooms. It was 6:00 P.M. and already pitch black outside. A storm had blown in earlier that afternoon, and soft flakes the size of goose feathers were piling up on the bushes surrounding the church. It was the final day of 2019, and soon church members would begin to arrive for the New Year's Eve celebration that would go on until a little past midnight.

The kitchen was filled with snacks, soft drinks, and coffee. The praise and worship band was warming up for their concert, and the workers from the children's ministry were laying out games and DVDs to entertain the little ones.

James had been concerned when the weather had turned bad. His initial thought was that people would stay away because of the snow, but the pastor had assured him that even though snow was nearly unheard of in San Antonio, the congregation would turn out for their eagerly anticipated New Year's Eve party.

James had come up with the idea of dropping a ball to signal the end of the year. When he was a child, his parents had allowed him to stay up to see the ball dropped in Times Square and to hear Dick Clark proclaim, "Happy New Year!"

James had always believed that one day he would be standing with the crowd in Times Square with a pretty girl holding his hand. When the ball dropped, he would kiss her and the television cameras would capture the moment. His mom and dad would be sitting at home watching when his face appeared on their television screen. They would be shocked to see him there looking devilishly handsome and sophisticated.

James had finished praying, and he began to turn up the thermostats to compensate for the dropping temperatures. Someone had turned on a radio, and a local weatherman was saying that most of the homeless people had gone into the shelters for protection against the harsh weather. James made a mental note to make the rounds of the shelters in the morning to make certain that they had enough supplies to accommodate the crowds.

James was not exactly happy, but he was content. He had grown in his relationship with Jesus, and each day he experienced some of the joy that comes from knowing Christ. He felt fulfilled in many respects, but that pretty girl whom he had always imagined would be part of his life had never materialized. Even now, he sometimes thought that if it had not been for Tracer, he would have married Macy, but even though he had always thought that she was the best girl he had ever known, he also knew that they were not right for each other. Macy and Tracer were a perfect match.

Billy was now semi-retired and Tracer had taken on most of the responsibilities of the construction company. He had earned a good reputation as an honest and talented builder, and under his leadership the company was expanding into various real-estate related fields.

Macy had begun nursing school the fall semester after she and Tracer had married, and she had been an RN for several years now. With her cheery personality and warm heart, she found many friends among the staff and the patients at the hospital, but, aside from her nursing duties, she felt that the best thing about being a nurse was the witnessing opportunities that opened up for her. When people are sick and dying, they often begin to look for answers, and that search opened doors for Macy to share Jesus with those who were willing to listen.

The door swung open admitting a blast of freezing air, and Macy entered the fellowship hall holding a pink blanket covering a baby girl with red curls and green eyes.

"How's Rosie?" James asked.

"She's good. She watched the snow through the window all the way over here."

"Where's Tracer?"

"He's bringing our stuff from the truck. He told me to get Rosie in here where it's warm. He's got all of her stuff and the buffalo wings and cookies."

"I'll help him," James responded as he stepped through the door onto the cold parking lot. The wet spots where the snow had melted earlier were freezing. James felt a twinge of concern as he thought about this parking lot filled with cars driven by people who had no idea of how to drive on ice.

By 6:30 the fellowship hall was packed. People were milling around talking and laughing with the easy familiarity of those who have known one another for years. The praise and worship band was playing loudly and competing with the congregation to be heard.

James was in charge of tonight's celebration, and he leapt onto the stage and picked up the microphone. "May I have your attention? Guys? Hello! Attention, please. I need to make a couple of announcements."

When the crowd grew quiet, James began to speak, "Tonight we're going to drop a ball to signal the arrival of the New Year. The youth designed and made it, and they did a great job!"

James began to applaud and the congregation applauded with him.

"Carson, bring that ball up here," James continued.

A skinny boy of about sixteen ascended the steps leading to the platform where the podium stood. He was carrying a ball about twelve inches in diameter that was covered in plastic "crystals" from the hobby store.

"Now, Carson, that's one fine looking ball!" James said enthusiastically. "I want everyone who worked on it to raise your hands."

The hands of five teenage girls shot into the air as they smiled and danced about, and more applause rang out.

James was holding the ball high in the air for the congregation to see. "The best thing about this ball," he continued, "is that it comes apart in the middle. And that isn't by mistake. I want everyone here to write one thing on a piece of paper that you want to get out of your life. Don't sign your paper. God knows who you are. We're going to pass around a bucket, and everyone is going to put his piece of paper in the bucket. Then we're going to put all of those pieces of paper into the ball and screw it shut. When it drops at midnight, I want you to give that thing that you wrote on your paper to God, and I want you to believe that with His help, it has left your life. There are note pads and pencils on the chairs, so get started."

The congregation began writing their notes to God asking Him to help them rid themselves of one particular thing in their lives. Some of the notes covered both sides of the paper, but James' note consisted of only one word, "Loneliness."

Chapter 35

Molly surveyed the dry brown landscape as she and Miguel neared the San Antonio city limits. She would have never believed that she would ever have returned to Texas to live, but she had few options. She could not pay the rent on her apartment on what she made as a Cocktail. Her tips were not what they used to be; the hot spots wanted Cocktails that were eighteen or nineteen, and her twenty-sixth birthday was right around the corner. She had been reduced to working in bars where she was lucky to get a five dollar tip, and she had to have a roommate. She could not bear the idea of sharing her apartment with another female, so when Miguel's father had a stroke the first week of January and his mother asked him to come back and run the family bar, she had agreed to make the move with him.

The plan was for him to tend bar and her to wait tables. Molly knew that the small bar was situated in a run-down part of town where many of the business people lived above their stores. Miguel had told her that his parents lived in the two rooms over the bar, but none of that concerned her. She and Miguel would get their own place in a few days, and after that she would not have to put up with his parents.

When Miguel parked her badly dented and dinged BMW in front of the bar, however, she was unprepared for the filth and poverty of the neighborhood. It was a cold day, even for January 8, and a brisk wind was blowing trash along the cracked sidewalks. A group of four or five small ragged children ran along the sidewalk laughing and pushing each other. A girl of six years danced up and down to keep her bare feet off the cold pavement as much as possible. As she continued her dance, she pressed her face up against the glass of the bar and called "Papa!" This was followed by a stream of Spanish. Apparently, she had been sent to tell her father to come home, but she did not wait for a response, and taking the hand of one of the younger children, she ran down the alley that separated the bar from its neighboring store and disappeared.

Molly was disturbed by the sight of the children in their thin cotton dresses with the wind whipping around their bare legs. "You'd think their mom would make them put on their coats," she said.

"They probably haven't got no coats," Miguel responded.

"Everybody has a coat!"

"That shows what you rich white chicks know!"

"I know that there are dozens of agencies that give kids all kinds of things."

"You don't know nothing, so shut up!"

Molly was cold, tired, and hungry. Her throat was sore, and she was so congested that she could hardly breathe. She pulled her own coat tighter around her and shivered as she stepped from the car. She looked at the faded wooden sign on the bar. The words *La Paloma Blanca* were painted in script across the board, and the peeling image of a white dove poised for flight adorned the upper right-hand corner.

"The White Dove?" Molly asked.

"What about it?"

"I don't know. It just seems like a weird name for a bar. My parents used to work in a ministry in Dallas that was called The White Dove. You know, like the dove of the Holy Spirit? Most people think of doves as being symbols of the Holy Spirit."

"I told you to shut up!" Miguel shouted.

He opened the ill-fitting wooden door of the bar and walked in ahead of her, ignoring her completely.

A woman of about fifty was behind the bar, and she turned toward the door when it opened. When she caught sight of Miguel, a wide smile brightened her face.

"Mijo!" she exclaimed as she came out from behind the bar and threw her arms around Miguel, kissing him repeatedly.

Miguel's mother ignored Molly so completely that, at first, Molly wondered whether she had seen her in the dim light. But, after she finished greeting Miguel, she turned to survey Molly with an icy stare that said that she had not only seen her but had sized her up and decided that she did not like her.

Miguel's mother placed her hands on her hips and stared at Molly. Then, with a jerk of her head, she motioned for Molly to follow her into a back room with a filthy cement floor and a rickety wooden staircase. The woman climbed the stairs ahead of Molly. When they had reached the top, they were standing in a tiny room with a few pieces of dilapidated furniture and a hotplate sitting on a decaying wooden cabinet that Miguel's grandfather had brought with him from Mexico.

"Put your stuff there," the woman said in heavily accented English as she pointed to a corner of the room.

Molly threw her canvas bag into the corner and turned to go back down the stairs.

"Flaca!" Miguel's mother said, "Don't try to give me no trouble."

Molly did not answer but descended the stairs and returned to the bar.

"What does 'Flaca' mean?"

"Huh?"

"Your mom called me 'Flaca.' What does it mean?"

"It means you, so don't worry about it."

It was growing dark, and the bar was filling up with men from the neighborhood. They were mostly older men with thick graying hair and mustaches and heavily-lined faces that made them appear tired and hopeless. They talked among themselves but did not speak to Molly. When they wanted another drink, they shouted their orders to Miguel who then told Molly what to take to which table. At first Molly thought that their lack of communication with her was the result of the language barrier, but as she observed the patrons, she realized that their refusal to speak to her went much deeper. She was an outsider, and they wanted her to know that they would never accept her. She was the enemy, a white girl who thought that she was too good for them, and they were going to prove to her that they could make her life miserable.

Although the men pretended to ignore Molly, their eyes followed her as she made her way through the narrow space delivering tecate and tequila to the small crowded tables. She was accustomed to taking care of herself, and she was normally not intimidated by drunks, but this was different. In the eyes of the men sitting in the bar she recognized a combination of hatred and lust that made her go cold with fear.

When the bar finally closed at 2:30 A.M., Molly stumbled up the stairs to go to bed. Her head was pounding, and she was certain that she was running a temperature. Miguel walked over to the couch and pulled out the lumpy mattress that converted it to a "sleeper." Molly had spent the entire evening thinking about getting into bed and wrapping up in a blanket, but the bed was so uncomfortable that she was certain that she would not be able to sleep at all. Miguel took the only blanket—a tattered, badly stained quilt and wrapped it around himself.

Molly rolled off the bed and retrieved her bag from the corner of the room. She pulled out a pair of sweat pants and some leggings and put them on. Then she pulled on a turtleneck sweater, put on her coat, and lay back down on the bed. Her last thought was, "I'll never be able to go to sleep."

The next thing Molly knew the sun was streaming through the window and shining directly into her eyes. She swallowed and a sharp pain stabbed her badly swollen tonsils. She was burning with fever, and she felt so weak that she was not certain that she could sit up.

Miguel's mother entered the room, and with an angry look, addressed her, "Get up, Flaca!"

Molly closed her eyes and rolled over. Instantly, a man's hand grabbed her arm, and she felt herself being dragged from the bed. She hit the bare floor with a thud. As she lay there she heard a woman's laughter, and she opened her eyes to see an expression of pure joy on Miguel's mother's face.

Miguel was behind the bar, and three old men were sitting at a table in the corner drinking and reminiscing about a better time when they were young and the women were beautiful.

Molly had managed to pull herself together and make her way down the stairs. She looked very thin and pale in her short skirt and tight sweater. She slowly made her way to the bar and seated herself on one of the stools. Miguel was pacing nervously, and it was apparent that he was feeling confrontational.

"Do you have a Coke back there?" Molly asked.

"No, I don't have no Cokes. What do you think this is, McDonalds?"

"I'm sick. I thought a Coke would help."

"Oh, isn't that too bad? If you don't stop complaining, I'm gonna give you something to complain about. And let me tell you something else; you better lay off my mom. You're gonna treat her with respect, you understand?"

"What are you talking about? I haven't said two words to your mother."

"Well, you better start treatin' her good or you're gonna wish you had."

"Miguel, I have flu, or strep throat, or something. I feel like I'm gonna die. Leave me alone."

Miguel was now in a rage, and he jumped over the bar, grabbed Molly's arm and began raining blows down on her head and chest. The men at the table watched with little interest as he continued to beat her until she was unconscious. Then, taking her by the hair, he opened the door and threw her limp body onto the sidewalk.

Chapter 36

Officer Roberto "Beto" Silva was driving his Cruiser west on Alameda when he saw the crumpled body of a young woman lying on the sidewalk between La Paloma Blanca and the alley. He quickly turned on his emergency lights and pulled to the curb. As he bent over the body, he knew at once that she was not from the neighborhood.

Beto called for an ambulance and checked to see whether he could find a pulse. He was surprised to discover that although the day was cold, the young woman's skin was hot to the touch. She was alive, but she had been severely beaten. Beto pulled a blanket from the trunk of his car and covered her; he knew that she was in danger of going into shock, and if she did, she might not survive.

La Paloma Blanca was situated less than five miles from the county hospital, and the ambulance arrived at the scene in under ten minutes. After the woman had been loaded into the ambulance, Beto began to look for witnesses. He opened the door of the bar and surveyed the three patrons still sitting at the table near the back.

"Anybody here know what happened to the woman on the sidewalk?" Beto asked looking directly at Miguel.

"What woman?" Miguel replied.

"The woman that someone beat unconscious and left outside your door."

"I didn't see nothin'. You guys see anything?" Miguel asked.

The three old men shook their heads and shrugged their shoulders.

"Come on, someone nearly killed her. She must have screamed. You must have heard something."

Again the old men shook their heads.

Beto turned toward Miguel, "You must have heard her."

"Not me. She's probably one of the crack whores that does business in the alley."

Beto knew that he was not going to get any information from Miguel or the patrons of the bar. He would have to wait until the girl was able to talk to him.

Molly opened her swollen eyes. She hurt all over, but she realized at once that she was in a warm clean bed. A woman's voice spoke to her. With effort Molly turned her head in the direction of the sound. A smiling face surrounded by bright red curls was peering down at her.

"I'm praying for you," the face said.

Molly barely nodded her head before her eyes closed, and she slipped back into a troubled sleep.

When Molly opened her eyes again, it was dark outside, and the only light in the room came from a dim overhead lamp attached to her bed. With great effort she turned her head and looked for the call button. Finally, she saw it attached to her bed rail, and taking it in her left hand, she rang for the nurse.

In a couple of minutes a chubby woman with mousey brown hair pulled straight back and wound into a little bun on the back of her head came through the door. She was artificially cheery, and exclaimed much louder than necessary, "Are you feeling better?"

Molly ignored her question. "How did I get here?"

"An ambulance brought you in at 1:00 this afternoon."

"Who called the ambulance?"

"I don't have any information about that. I can call for the counselor, and she can tell you more."

"Call her. Can I have something to drink? I'm really thirsty."

The chubby nurse reached for a small plastic pitcher filled with crushed ice and water at Molly's bedside, poured the cold water into a small plastic glass, and handed it to Molly.

"Will you raise my bed?"

The nurse obediently pressed a button that raised the bed until Molly's head was high enough for her to drink without spilling water on herself. When Molly took a sip of the cold water, she winced. "This tastes terrible!"

"It's your meds; they make things taste kind of funny."

"Look, I'm really thirsty, but I can't drink this. Can I get a Coke?"

"How about a Sprite? We don't have Coke."

"Okay, I'll take a Sprite."

The chubby nurse hurried away leaving Molly alone in the dimly lit room. As she looked about, she saw a clock on the wall. It was 8:00 P.M. She could hear the visitors leaving the rooms of the patients as a different nurse made her way down the hall telling them that visiting hours had ended.

It was 8:30 before Molly's Sprite arrived. She hated Sprite, but she was so thirsty that she was determined to drink it anyway. She took a few sips and placed the can with the straw in it on her bedside table.

A tiny Asian woman in her mid-thirties entered the room. She was dressed in civilian clothes and was carrying a clipboard with forms attached. She smiled as she took her place next to the chair on the left side of Molly's bed, but she did not sit.

"My name is Karen. I'm a counselor here at the hospital, and I need to get a statement from you."

"Get out of here," Molly responded. "How's that for a statement?"

"That's pretty funny," Karen responded. "I see that you're a comedian. Did someone beat you up because they didn't like your comedy routine?"

Molly did not answer.

"Who did this to you?"

"Nobody. I fell"

"Wow! You really are a comedian!"

Molly refused to say anything else, and after a few minutes, Karen left her room.

∞

The following morning Officer Silva entered Molly's hospital room.

When Molly saw the uniform, she nearly panicked. Her first thought was that he had come to arrest her. She hadn't done anything, but her lifestyle had resulted in several brushes with the law, and now every time she saw a police uniform, her heart beat a little faster.

Beto was surprised to see that she was very pretty—almost beautiful. In fact, he was certain that if she were not so bruised and battered, she would be a show stopper. When he spoke, however, he was careful to remain professional in his questioning and attitude.

After introducing himself, he asked, "Can you tell me what happened?"

Molly stared at him but did not answer. Then she turned her eyes toward the window, hoping that he would leave.

"Ma'am, I need to find out who hurt you."

"Nobody. I don't remember."

"Were you in La Paloma Blanca earlier yesterday?"

"No."

"Where were you?"

"I don't remember."

"Where do you live?"

"I don't remember."

"Is your name Molly Anderson?"

Beto noted that Molly started when he spoke her name, but rather than answering his question, she laid her head back on her pillows and closed her eyes.

"Molly, I can't help you if you won't talk to me."

Molly lay motionless with her eyes closed.

After a few more attempts to get a response from her, Beto said, "I'm leaving my card here on your table. If you remember anything, call me."

When Molly opened her eyes again, Officer Silva was gone, and the nurse with the red curls was adjusting her IV bag.

The nurse's beautiful pink lips curved into a smile, "How are you feeling?"

"Grim."

"Can I get you something?"

"How about a Coke?"

"I'll ask the doctor."

Molly was certain that the bubbly red head would not ask the doctor. Ten minutes later, however, an aide came in carrying an unopened can of Coke and a glass of crushed ice.

"What's the nurse's name?" Molly asked.

"Which one?"

"The one with the red hair."

"Oh, that's Macy."

Molly opened the Coke and filled the glass to the brim. Lifting it high she said, "Here's to you Macy," and took a long drink.

Early the next morning Macy entered Molly's room smiling brightly.

"The doctor's going to release you some time before noon. Your temperature's normal, and nothing's broken. You don't have any internal injuries, so you're good to go. Do you want me to call someone to pick you up?"

Molly was unprepared for the news that she was about to be released from the hospital, and she was suddenly more frightened than she had been for a long time.

"No."

"Do you have family or friends here?" Macy asked.

"No."

"Do you have somewhere to go?"

"No."

"You are going to need to get some rest. You were pretty sick when you came in here. The antibiotics knocked out the infection, but it will be a few days before you're a hundred percent. If you don't have anywhere to go, I can get you into the battered women's shelter. I volunteer there, and it's a good place. You'd probably be surprised to learn how many women are trapped in abusive relationships because they have nowhere to go. The shelter gives them a place to stay while they are learning some skills and finding jobs."

"No, Thanks!" Molly replied more forcefully than she had intended.

"Where will you go?" Macy inquired further.

"That's my business."

"I have someone I would like you to talk to. If I call him, will you talk to him before you leave the hospital?"

In spite of her tough act, Molly's mind was racing, trying to think what she should do. "I guess."

"Okay, I'm going to call him now, and when he arrives, I'll bring him in."

Chapter 37

Molly had showered and dressed when Macy next entered her hospital room. With her scrubbed face and freshly shampooed hair falling loose around her shoulders, she looked young and fragile.

"Molly, this is James Goodwin, the guy I told you about. If the doctor comes in while he's here, James will wait in the hall until he's gone and then come back in."

Molly was surprised at James' appearance. She had expected an old guy with glasses who smelled like Listerine. James was about her age, and he was wearing jeans and a Dallas Cowboys jacket. He was small and fine boned with thick light brown hair and hazel eyes. The hand that he extended when Macy introduced them was not much bigger than hers.

Molly took a seat in one of the visitor's chairs in her room and James sat in the other. She felt self-conscious as she faced him.

"I'm a mess," she said as she nervously twisted a long piece of blonde hair. "I lost my make-up."

"You look fine," James answered as casually as he could. In truth, he was mesmerized by this beautiful young woman who seemed so vulnerable and alone.

James had dated several women since becoming a Christian, but they were girls whose main interest was in catching a husband. They were nice girls, but they wanted to find a man to marry who would support them and any children they might have. They had definite ideas about the roles of wives and husbands, but they did not seem to be very interested in him. They were convinced that as long as they married another Christian, God would take care of the rest. Any of them would have married him, but none of them was in love with him.

James was careful not to let Molly know that he was attracted to her, but as he looked into those sad blue eyes, he knew that, if he were not careful, he would fall in love with her.

James made Molly feel safe; she sensed a gentleness about him that she had never known in a man. Her father was protective and loving but tough; Dustin had been non-confrontational, but he was needy and a whiner. Her other boyfriends had been rough macho types who were well able to "protect" her but were just as likely to smack her around if she got in their way.

James was small and soft-spoken. Like many people who love to perform for audiences, he was unsure of himself in one-on-one situations. As he sat talking quietly to her, Molly began to relax. She felt that in his presence she would never have to fear anything. It wasn't so much that he was capable of protecting her; it was that she believed he would never put her in a situation where she would be in danger.

Molly found herself talking to James more openly than she would have believed possible. While she did not give him any specifics, she told him that her boyfriend was responsible for her injuries. She also admitted to him that she did not have anywhere to go.

"Will your mom and dad let you stay with them?"

"I can't go there," Molly replied. "They would never understand."

"Will you go into the battered women's shelter for a few days until we can help you get a job?"

Molly heard herself agreeing to James' request. As soon as she did so, she wanted to take it back, but she was out of options.

"I have to go now," James said as he rose to his feet. "Macy will get you settled at the shelter. Tomorrow we have CR at the church. Will you come?

"What's CR?"

"It's a twelve-step recovery program. I'm one of the leaders."

"You mean for addicts and like that?"

"Yeah, will you come?"

"I'm not an addict," Molly responded defensively.

"Will you come anyway? It isn't just for addicts; it's also for people who are in abusive relationships."

"Maybe."

"I'll take that as a 'yes'," James said smiling. "Friday is spaghetti night. I'll save you a place."

Chapter 38

Friday morning dawned cold and gray. During the night a storm had covered everything with a layer of crystal clear ice that made any sort of travel precarious but which provided a glistening winter wonderland for those who were fortunate enough to be able to stay close to home.

Elizabeth sat at the round mahogany table in the breakfast nook of the large Tuscan-style kitchen of the lake house sipping a cup of scalding tea and watching the birds perched on the telephone wires in the field behind the house. Boomer was still sleeping under the white goose down comforter that covered the bed in the master suite, but Elizabeth had been up since 4:30.

The two of them had arrived the night before for an extended weekend. Boomer had worked long hours to finish up several projects before the New Year, and he was tired. Elizabeth had thought that it would be good for both of them to spend their three-day weekend napping, reading, and eating. She was surprised, therefore, when she had been unable to sleep. Every time she dozed off she would awake with a start and begin thinking about Molly. She lay in bed and prayed for her until she realized that she should probably get up and go into the great room where she could pray aloud.

Molly had dominated Elizabeth's thoughts all week. It wasn't just that she thought about her—she thought about her every day, but this week whenever Molly came to mind, Elizabeth felt uneasy—as if some unidentified menace were lurking in the shadows waiting to strike. She had spent hours praying for her daughter, but she had not received any assurance that the danger had passed. She had called Molly's cell phone, but it had gone directly to voice mail. When she had tried to e-mail her, the e-mail had bounced.

When she had told Boomer about her concern, he had replied that Molly would contact them when she was ready. "You know how she is," he had said. "She drops out of sight for months at a time, and then one day, out of the blue, she calls. She probably changed her e-mail address. Her cell is still active, so I wouldn't worry too much."

Elizabeth knew that Boomer was probably right, but her intuition told her that Molly was in danger. In spite of the fire burning in the stacked stone fireplace tucked into one end of the kitchen, Elizabeth shivered. She pulled her oversized sweater around her more tightly and directed her attention to the field. The winter grass was golden, and the few trees were bare, but it was still a beautiful and serene refuge. Elizabeth thought about how the field would look in May when the wildflowers were in full bloom and the deep green grass was a foot high.

She would come back then and walk the familiar paths that she and the girls had explored when they were growing up. She wondered how many times the three of them had picked wildflowers to fill vases for the dinner table. At the far corner of the field wild roses climbed an ancient wooden fence. Molly had especially loved the pale pink blooms, and the summer that she was eight she had plucked their short stems and carried them home in a rusty bucket that they found abandoned near a little stream. The memory was so painful that hot tears welled up in Elizabeth's eyes, and she did not hear Boomer enter the kitchen.

"You're up early," he said.

Elizabeth started, "Oh! You scared me!"

"I'm sorry. I woke up and you were gone. It's only 6:30. Couldn't you sleep?"

"No, I'm still worried about Molly."

"Well, Sugar, there's nothing we can do except pray for her."

"I have been praying for her all week, and last night I spent so much time praying for her that I didn't sleep at all. I'm so worried."

"Lizzie, you're going to have to trust the Lord to take care of her."

"I know. It's just hard sometimes."

"What's for breakfast?" Boomer asked.

"How about cheeseburgers?" Elizabeth suggested.

"Sounds good to me. I'll put on the coffee."

Elizabeth felt better as the sky grew lighter and she and Boomer sat eating their cheeseburgers and drinking coffee. Elizabeth had never liked the traditional breakfast foods, but she considered cheeseburgers hot from her own kitchen served with freshly ground coffee to be the perfect way to begin the day.

After a quick clean-up, Elizabeth asked Boomer if he wanted to go for a walk with her.

"It's cold outside!" he exclaimed. "I'm going to build a fire in the great room and catch a football game. You ought to stay in too. It's slick out there."

"I'll be careful; I have my rubber-soled boots. I need some fresh air."

Elizabeth entered the field by ducking and passing between the large wooden rails that comprised the fence. Once inside she took a familiar path that led to the corner with the wild roses. The cold air stung her nose, but she was glad to be walking alone in this place where she had spent so many happy hours with her girls.

"Dear Lord," she said aloud, "what am I supposed to do? I've prayed for Molly for such a long time, but she seems to just be getting worse. If I were a bad mother to her, please forgive me. I thought that I was doing all the right things, and I thought that she knew how much her dad and I loved her, but something was wrong or she wouldn't have ended up the way she did. I wanted more than anything for my girls to grow up to love you and to serve you, and I tried to teach them about you and to set a good example for them, but I failed with Molly. Please forgive me."

Tears were streaming down Elizabeth's face, which was already red from the cold. Her nose was beginning to run, and the freezing air caused her ears to ache, but she quickened her pace and continued on the path to the wild rose bushes.

When she reached the corner, she stood looking at the tangle of dry brown stems that covered an area about eight feet wide and climbed to the height of the fence. As Elizabeth surveyed the rose bushes, she thought that there is nothing sadder looking than a dormant plant waiting for the warm spring sun to call it back to life. No one would ever believe that this jumble of dry sticks and brown leaves could ever become something beautiful and fragrant. Yet, she knew that when she made this walk in the spring all traces of death and decay would have been swept away, and the pale pink blossoms with their intoxicating perfume would once again fill this corner.

Elizabeth had never been able to look at the wild roses without thinking of the eight-year-old Molly with her flaxen hair and cornflower eyes carrying the rusty pail filled to the brim with the delicate blooms. She smiled through her tears as she remembered how Molly had cut the stems so short that they could not put them in a vase. Elizabeth had looked through the cabinets and found a large shallow pasta bowl in creamy white porcelain. She and Molly had filled it with water and floated the blooms on the surface. They had placed it in the middle of the table at dinnertime, and Boomer had said that it was the most beautiful centerpiece he had ever seen. Molly had glowed with pride as she told him how she had found the flowers and carried them home all by herself.

As Elizabeth stood looking at the dead bushes, she realized that Molly was like these roses. She had entered into a spiritual winter where it seemed to the observer that every trace of the beautiful young woman, so full of promise, had disappeared. But, like the roses, Molly's spirit was waiting to be called back to life. As she stood reflecting on all that had happened, the words, "Trust me; trust me; trust me," repeated themselves in Elizabeth's head.

After a long time, Elizabeth said out loud, "Yes, Lord, I will trust you."

Slowly Elizabeth walked back to the house. It was beginning to snow—tiny flakes that blew in the wind and stung her face. But for the first time that week, Elizabeth felt calm. When she arrived at the house, she joined Boomer in the great room where he was fixated on his football game. Curling up on the oversized sofa, she pulled a large chenille throw over her, closed her eyes, and entered into a peaceful sleep.

Chapter 39

*A*t 6:00 on Friday evening James was nervously pacing the fellowship hall, biting his fingernails and checking out the door every time anyone entered. He forced himself to chat with the other CR leaders as well as those attending the groups. He was practicing looking nonchalant and trying to decide how he would greet Molly without seeming too pleased to see her. Tony had been talking for several minutes, but James had not heard a word he had said.

"So, what do you think?" Tony asked.

"Oh, uh, I think that sounds great." James replied.

"You think it's great that we may have to move CR out of the church in order to maintain our tax exempt status?"

"No. No, I think...."

Just then the door opened, and James' eyes turned toward the sound. Molly entered the room wearing the same skirt and sweater she had been wearing the previous day. The shelter had given her a puffy purple jacket that was too big for her, and standing there in her short skirt and oversized coat she reminded James of Alice when she had fallen down the rabbit hole and encountered the drink that made her grow and the cookie that made her shrink. Molly's skirt and sweater looked too small, but her coat swallowed her, so James was trying to decide whether she was now too big or too small for her clothes.

Just then Molly spotted him and flashed a smile that made his heart leap. She had brushed her long blonde hair into a pony tail with long pale wisps softly framing her face. She was still bruised, but Macy had covered most of the discolorations with makeup and put a little pale pink gloss on her lips and a touch of mascara on her lashes.

Macy, who was standing behind Molly, saw the look on James' face and knew that if she played her cards right, she could be a matchmaker. "Hey, James!" Macy called. "Come over here!"

Quickly, James moved toward the two young women.

"I've got to take Rosie to the nursery," Macy said. "Can you keep Molly company and get her some food?"

"Sure," James replied. "I'm glad you could make it," he said looking at Molly. He continued looking directly into Molly's eyes as he placed his hand on her arm and directed her to the serving line.

When they had their food and were seated, James introduced Molly to the other people at the table and made small talk with them. He wished desperately that he could sit at a table alone with her and find out everything about her, but that was not possible. He was a church leader; he was involved in men's ministry. Molly would be placed in a group with women. He would probably never be able to talk to her again!

James noticed that after her first taste of her spaghetti, Molly had not eaten anything else. She sipped the tea but left her plate untouched.

When the meal ended and the tables had been cleared away, James leaned close to Molly and whispered softly in her ear, "Don't worry, we'll get you a burger after the meeting. I remember what it was like the first time I ate spaghetti here."

Molly had laughed out loud, and for the first time, James saw a glint of humor in her eyes.

Macy introduced Molly to Donna Dawson and told her that she was going to be in Donna's group. James watched as the three women turned and walked away, Macy to practice for praise and worship and Molly and Donna to the women's CR room.

It seemed to James that the following two hours would never end. It was with the greatest effort that he forced himself to listen to the group members and fulfill his role as their leader. He kept wondering whether he would ever see Molly again after tonight, and he felt that he could not stand the thought of losing her so soon after having found her.

When the men's group ended, James hurried into the hallway to see whether the women's group had already let out. He walked to the door and listened. He could hear female voices; they were still talking. Quickly, James moved away from the door and headed back toward his CR room. Standing just inside the doorway, he waited until he heard the women's door open. He took a deep breath and paused until he heard Molly's voice in the hallway. His timing was perfect; he stepped into the hallway when Molly was still about three feet from the door.

"Hey," James said trying to act surprised to see her. "How'd it go?"

"It went okay."

James saw Tracer and Macy approaching from the far end of the hallway. Tracer was carrying Rosie, who was sound asleep in her baby seat.

"Tracer!" James called. "I promised Molly a burger. I'm going to give you the money for all of you to go eat—my treat."

Molly, looked startled, "Aren't you coming with us?" she inquired.

"Well, I guess I could..."

Macy smiled sweetly. "Rosie's asleep, and I don't want to wake her. Would you two mind if Tracer and I took her on home, and you two went without us?"

James quickly looked at Molly to see her reaction. She smiled and nodded in agreement.

It was settled. James and Molly were about to go on their first date.

Chapter 40

$\mathcal{J}$ames held open the door to Big Bob's Burgers and Molly walked inside. It was a local diner with a retro '50s vibe. With its black and white checkerboard floor and red vinyl booths with their Formica tops, it looked like something out of the old *Happy Days* television series that James had watched in reruns when he was growing up. Posters of Elvis, Jerry Lee Lewis, and Ricky Nelson decorated the walls, and waitresses in pink '50s style uniforms waited the tables.

When they were seated and had ordered, James asked Molly to tell him about herself.

"You first," she replied.

"Not much to tell," James responded. "I've been going to the church for nine years. I'm a CR leader, and I play in the praise and worship band. During the day, I'm in charge of finishing and detail for Ferguson Building Corporation. I like my job, and I like my work at the church."

"What's finishing and detail?"

"I started as a painter, but pretty soon Billy, the owner, decided that I had a good eye for detail. He gave me the job of making sure that everything on each project was finished correctly. I, actually, love what I do. There's something wonderful about being part of a project from the ground up and seeing it come together perfectly."

Molly winced.

"What's the matter?" James asked.

"Nothing. You sound like my dad."

"Is that bad?"

"Depends on who you ask. Tell me about the band."

James launched into a lengthy discussion of his experiences with the praise and worship band, and when he told Molly about being chased by a pack of dogs when they were attempting to play a concert in the park as an evangelistic tool, she laughed so hard that James wondered whether she was putting him on.

"It's not that funny," James finally said.

"It is the way you tell it. You're a great storyteller!"

No one had ever told James that he was a good storyteller. He loved to tell stories to relate everyday events, but most people found his long drawn-out descriptions irritating. Molly was the first person who had ever appreciated his talent.

When the waitress finally came to their booth to tell them that the kitchen was closing in fifteen minutes, James was surprised. He looked at his watch and discovered that it was 10:45. He quickly paid the bill and escorted Molly back to his new Chevy truck. He was glad that he had gotten the truck before he met her. Even though she had not told him anything about herself, James had the feeling that she was accustomed to nice things.

When they arrived at the shelter, they sat in the truck and talked. Molly was in no hurry to go inside, and she asked him, "Do you have a girlfriend?"

"No, not right now."

"Why not? You're hot."

"Most girls don't like my rules."

Molly gave him her most flirtatious look. "Ohhh, that sounds interesting."

James suddenly looked very serious. "Soon after I got saved, Pastor Brian brought the *True Love Waits* program to the church. Have you ever heard of it?"

"Oh, Yeah. When I was a kid, my parents tried to get me to make a purity pledge at our church. They twisted my little sister's arm, and she did the pledge, the ring, the whole thing. I told them that I didn't need to take a pledge and wear a ring to stay pure, and they finally backed off."

"In my case, I did need to take a pledge to stay pure," James said. "I was considered too old for the program, which was aimed at teens, but I privately promised God that from that day forward I would remain celibate until I was married. I bought this cross and put it around my neck as a symbol of my vow, and I have never taken it off."

"You're a virgin?" Molly asked.

"No. I was pretty wild before I gave my heart to Jesus, but when He forgave me, that old person died. I know that as far as God is concerned, I'm now washed clean because of my faith in Jesus Christ. Have you seen any of those television ads for Second Virginity? They're for people like me who've made a lot of mistakes but see the error of their ways and change their lives. When I became a new creature in Christ, I had a chance to start clean, and I took it.

"Girls don't care much for guys who won't have sex with them. Even a lot of the girls in the church sleep with their boyfriends, and they don't want to be involved with someone who is saving sex for marriage."

Molly tried not to look shocked. She had really liked James. She had thought that they had a connection, but this was creepy.

"I better go inside," she said at last as she opened the passenger side door and hopped down into the street.

James walked her to the door and said goodnight.

"James, can I give you a little goodnight kiss?"

"No. Will you come to church Sunday morning? I'll pick you up at 8:30."

"I'm not sure I can make it."

"I'm sure, and I'll be here, so be waiting for me exactly where you're standing now."

When James arrived at the shelter on Sunday morning, Molly was standing exactly where he had left her, but her hair hung loosely down her back, reaching almost to her waist. She looked fresh and young and beautiful. James felt his heart leap when she smiled in the direction of his truck.

When she was inside and they were headed toward the church, Molly said, "After church can I talk to you about something?"

"Sure," James replied. "Can you tell me now?"

"I guess. The thing is, I have a problem. My car is at my boyfriend's house and I need to get it back, but I don't have my keys, and I'm afraid to go over there alone. So will you go with me?"

"Is it your car? Are you on title alone?"

"My dad and I are on title. He bought it for me for my high school graduation. My dad has the title. He paid cash for it so it's been paid for forever."

"What kind of car is it?"

"A BMW. It's got a lot of miles on it, but it still runs really well."

"Was it new when your dad gave it to you?"

"Of course, it was new! Do you think my dad would give me a used car?" Molly sounded indignant.

"I don't know. It has happened."

"It didn't happen to me. Anyway, I need my car, so can you get it for me?"

"Maybe. Probably. Let me think about how to do it, and I'll let you know."

"When?"

"Tomorrow."

Chapter 41

When James arrived at the job site on Monday morning, he was glad to see Billy's truck parked near the on-site office trailer. Opening the door to the office, James stuck his head inside and said, "Good morning, Billy! You're just the man I want to see."

Billy's face lighted in his perpetual smile. "Well, come on in!" he responded, obviously delighted to see James.

When James was seated in one of the dusty vinyl chairs across from Billy's gray metal desk, he told him everything he knew about Molly. He ended by saying, "I want to help her get her car back, but I'm not sure how to go about it. I think it could be dangerous if it isn't done right."

"You're right about that. You go over there and try to take that car, and you're likely to get your head blown off. I'll tell you what; I'll call John Taylor over at the bank and ask him who they use to do their repossessions. Are you willing to pay them to go over there and get it?"

"Sure!" James responded, obviously relieved that he wouldn't be put in a position where he might come to blows with the ex-boyfriend.

After a few calls Billy gave James the number to call to set up the repo. Since James was a "new customer" he was charged double the going rate, but he was so glad to have someone else do it that he didn't even try to negotiate the price.

James gave Bruce, the repo guy, the address of La Paloma Blanca and the license number of Molly's car. "It'll be parked in front of the bar," James said. "The bar closes at 2:30, and the owner lives upstairs so he won't be driving the car away. When can you do it?"

"I'll get it tonight. Do you want me to make you a set of keys too?"

"Yes, absolutely."

"That's another hundred dollars for two keys."

"I only need one key."

"Okay, that's another hundred dollars for one key. Where do you want it delivered?" Bruce asked.

James gave him the address of the church and told him to call him as soon as they had the car, and he would meet him there.

At 3:30 A.M. James received the call on his cell.

"We're on our way," Bruce mumbled. "Meet us there."

James had remained dressed so that he could leave as soon as the call came in. Jumping to his feet, he pulled on his jacket and headed out the door.

He arrived at the church at the same time as Bruce and his partner Larry. After giving them a check and taking the new key, James drove Molly's car around back to the area secured with a chain link fence topped with concertina wire where the church parked its vehicles. When the car was locked safely inside, James headed back to his apartment feeling victorious.

On his drive home James thought about Molly's car. It was a silver BMW Z4, a 2012 year model, but, in spite of the neglect, it still looked good—like a beautiful woman on hard times. She might not have been to the salon for a while, and she might be wearing sale rack clothes, but she still has beauty and class. That little Beemer still had beauty and class too; all she needed was a little love and a good body shop.

The following morning James called Macy and asked her to get in touch with Molly at the shelter and to tell her to call him about her car.

"What are you talking about?" Macy asked.

"She'll know," James responded. "Just tell her to call."

Within fifteen minutes James' cell rang. "James, its Molly. Do you have my car?"

"I don't know. I have me a 2012 silver BMW Z4. Does that sound like it could be your car?"

"Oh!" Molly squealed. "You rock!"

"Not so fast," James said. "I'm gonna need for you to identify it. What's the license number?"

"James, stop it!"

"Now, now, now, Ma'am. I can't be turning a fine automobile like this over to just anyone. I'll need the license number."

Molly decided to play along and repeated the number to James.

"Okay, I guess I'll let you have it. How do you want me to get it to you?"

"I don't know. I can't park it at the shelter. I'll have a job in a few days and get out of here. Can you hold onto it until then?"

"Don't worry. I've got it in a safe place. In the meantime, would you like a supervised visit?"

"Of course."

"I'll pick you up at 6:30 this evening and we can go get something to eat. If you're very good, afterwards I'll take you to see your girl."

Chapter 42

Molly lay on the small bed pushed up against one wall of her tiny efficiency apartment. She stared into the darkness as the sounds of passing traffic and distant sirens invaded her thoughts. She had left the shelter as soon as she had received her first paycheck, but she had been severely restricted in her choice of apartments; the only one she had found that she could afford was this 15 x 15 foot box with a tiny refrigerator, an ancient stove, and a bed that was about as comfortable as an ironing board.

The best thing about the apartment was its location; it was only a few blocks from the hospital. Macy had gotten her a job working there as an aide, and she found that she actually enjoyed the interaction with the patients. She dealt mostly with seniors who were having surgery and were more uncomfortable than sick. She liked making them laugh with her witty remarks, and she enjoyed working in a safe environment where she did not have to worry about being attacked by other employees or drunken customers.

Normally, after a long day on her feet, Molly was grateful to climb into bed and go to sleep, but tonight she felt wide awake. She missed the clubs. For the past six years she had spent every day in a bar or club—sometimes as a Cocktail and sometimes as a customer, but, in one way or another, the club scene had always been a part of her life. It had now been two months since she had awakened to find herself in that hospital bed, and she was restless. She did not want to continue to work in clubs, but she did want to be able to party on weekends.

Molly was looking forward to the end of the week. It was the first time since she had been employed at the hospital that she had been scheduled to have both Saturday and Sunday off. She could go to her CR meeting, be out by 9:00, and start hitting some of the hot spots. She felt a tingle of excitement as she lay in the dark room fantasizing about the up-coming weekend.

The only problem was James. He was cute, and if he hadn't been such a Jesus freak, he would have been sexy, but he was so bent on saving the world that he couldn't think about anything else. She had heard a little about his past— enough to know that he had once been a cool guy. If James were still cool, Molly would have moved in with him, but he had allowed Christianity to turn him into a little prude who didn't even want a good night kiss. She had teased him and flirted with him for weeks, but he had ignored her advances; it was time for her to move on and find herself a man who appreciated women. Still, she knew that he would be waiting for her after the CR meeting ended. They had gone out for burgers every Friday night since she had begun attending CR, and she would have to make up an excuse for not going.

Molly could feel herself growing drowsy. Just before she fell asleep she saw herself at four years old riding the Merry-go-Round at Six Flags. Boomer was standing next to her with his arm around her so that she wouldn't fall off. The memory was so vivid that she could smell his cologne and hear the sound of his laughter. She was seated on a white horse with pink reigns—she had told her dad before he put her on the ride that she had to ride that horse. She remembered exactly how she had felt when he had lifted her high into the air and set her on the pink saddle. Now, in her memory she was riding around and around while the music played and her long hair blew in the breeze. She felt safe and happy; as long as she was with her father, nothing bad could ever happen to her. A shot of adrenaline surged through her body; her eyes flew open, and she was wide awake.

Molly sat up and stared into the darkness. Her hands were shaking, and her throat felt dry. Tears began to fill her eyes and spill down her cheeks. She had no idea why she was crying or how long she sat weeping in the blackness, but after what seemed like a long time she slumped back onto her cot and slept until she was awakened by the sound of her alarm.

The next day was Friday, and Molly felt more certain than ever that what she needed was a night out. She had only a few dollars, but that was not a problem. Guys were always eager to buy her drinks. She enjoyed watching them work to impress her and vie for the privilege of taking her home with them. She had bought a few clothes, and since she wore a uniform at work, she had been able to steer clear of "professional" looking attire. Her wardrobe was limited, but it was hot and sexy.

She would be forced to wear something to CR that she could wear to the clubs afterwards and still not raise too many red flags. She chose a black spandex top and a skirt that was barely street legal. As she slipped into black stiletto heels with Roman straps, she felt like herself again—

beautiful, desirable, and in control. Putting on the puffy purple coat, she locked her apartment door and headed for her car.

When she arrived at the church, she was unaware that eyebrows raised when she took off her coat. She felt smug because she was about to run a con on everyone there, and that gave her a special rush that she had not experienced since she had landed in the hospital. She was especially sweet and friendly to all of the women. She hugged Macy, and Donna, and Betty, the pastor's wife. The only person she ignored was James. When she caught a glimpse of him out of the corner of her eye, she felt a pang of guilt, but she quickly reminded herself that it was his own fault. He had been given his chance, and he had blown it.

When dinner had ended and everyone had split up into their groups, Molly began to count the minutes until she would be able to leave. The only reason that she had continued to attend the group was because she had no friends in San Antonio. Now she realized that she was in a position to begin to meet new people and get away from CR and everything it represented.

Donna's voice pierced Molly's thoughts, "Tonight I want each of us to think about what's missing in our lives. Women's reasons for coming to CR are very different from men's. Some of us struggle with alcohol or drug addiction, but most of us are here because of self-esteem issues. We feel unloved, lonely, and empty. Most of us have been either abused or rejected by the men in our lives. But we all have a need, or we wouldn't be here. Tonight we are going to begin to identify the hurts and struggles in our lives so that we can begin healing...."

As Donna continued speaking, Molly recalled her experience on Thursday night when the memory of her father had been so overwhelming. Once again the scene came into her mind so vividly that she felt as if she were watching a film. Without warning her eyes filled with tears that spilled down her cheeks and splashed onto her blouse. Molly struggled to regain her composure before Donna spotted her. The last thing she needed was to be singled out for special prayer. The other women might be in CR because they had needs, but she was there only because of a series of unfortunate events. She had made a mistake in coming back to Texas. That's why she was remembering her childhood and her dad. She had gotten too close to Dallas.

When the meeting ended, Molly was the first one out the door. She was expecting to see James in the hall, but he was nowhere in sight. Although she wanted to avoid him, she wondered why he was not waiting for her. Quickly she walked to his CR room and peered through the partially opened door. The room was empty. She made her way back to the fellowship hall where he always went to tell everyone good-by before he turned out the lights and locked up. He was nowhere to be seen. Molly was beginning to feel angry. Where was he? How dare he just disappear like that!

Molly walked to her car in the cold night air and noticed that James' truck had already left the parking lot. "If you think you're going to dump me, you're wrong!" she said aloud. "I'm dumping you, Baby!"

Molly was still angry as she headed for the club district. She had been scouting the downtown area since she had gone to work at the hospital, and armed with the recommendations she had gotten from co-workers, she had decided that she would try *Pure Pleasure* first. It had just opened, and everyone complained that the lines were long, but she knew from experience that she could get the bouncers to let her in ahead of the others. She left the puffy purple coat in the car and braved the cold in her clubbing clothes. Sure enough, as soon as the head bouncer saw her approaching, he motioned for her to come up to the head of the line and unhooked the rope to let her pass. She gave him her biggest smile and paused to survey the room.

A few diners were finishing their meals in the restaurant portion, but all of the action was at the bar and on the dance floor. She headed for the bar, but before she arrived a big guy in an expensive suit and long hair slicked back in a ponytail asked her to dance. Sizing him up quickly, Molly guessed that he was into some sort of crime and would have plenty of cash to spend on a beautiful woman.

Molly smiled and took his hand. As he led her toward the dance floor, she stepped down wrong on her left foot, and the heel snapped off her shoe. She let out a little scream as she felt the tendons tear and a white-hot pain shoot through her ankle. Within seconds the ankle began to swell.

The big guy glanced down at her injured ankle, shrugged, and turned and walked away leaving her to navigate the crowd and hobble to the door. She had no choice but to take off her shoes and walk barefoot on the freezing pavement; she was in so much pain that she could hardly make it to her car. As she covered the distance, she thought about the barefoot children she had seen the day she had arrived. Compared to them, she was lucky. Opening the car door she reached for her coat.

"Come here you purple beast!" she said as she pulled it on and buttoned it tightly against the cold.

By the time Molly arrived at her apartment her ankle was badly swollen and had turned a purplish red color. She thought that she needed some sort of medical attention, but was unsure as to what she should do. When she had managed to get inside and seat herself on her cot, she phoned Macy and told her that she was afraid that her ankle was broken.

"I'll come right over," Macy responded.

As Molly sat in the cold room waiting for Macy, she again thought about her father. She wished he were with her; he would know what to do. He would take her to the emergency room and get her the medical attention she needed. Better yet, he would probably call Dr. Pace, his personal physician, and have him meet them at his office so that they wouldn't have to wait in the ER. Molly had wrapped herself in a blanket that she had bought on sale at Walmart, and in spite of the pain in her ankle, she nodded off while she waited for Macy's arrival. Twenty minutes later when she heard the knock at the door, she started and called out, "I'm coming!"

When she had unlocked the door and let Macy inside, she hobbled back to the cot. Macy pulled up a small straight-backed chair and said, "Let me see what we've got here."

"Where's James?" Macy asked as she gently held Molly's ankle between her hands and moved it carefully.

"I don't know."

"Don't you two go out on Friday nights?" Macy inquired.

"Sometimes. Not tonight."

"Are you arguing?"

"No."

"Did you break up?"

"He's not my boyfriend!"

"You don't like him?" Macy persisted.

"I hate him! He's a big jerk."

"That's too bad because I was going to call him to ask him to come over here and help me get you to the car. You shouldn't be walking on this. I don't think it's broken, but you need an x-ray."

Molly looked sullen. "What do you want me to do?" Macy asked.

"Call him."

When James arrived, he handed Molly her coat and then picked her up and carried her to his truck. She was as tall as he, and it was all he could do to carry her, but he would have rather died than let her know what a struggle it was get her to the truck. When he had deposited her inside, he walked to the rear of the truck and gasped for breath before continuing on to the driver's side.

Macy followed in her car, so the two of them were alone in the cab of the truck just as they had been on previous Friday evenings. Now, however, the atmosphere was strained.

"Don't you want to know what happened?" Molly asked.

"Not particularly," James replied.

"I stepped down, and my foot slipped. I twisted my ankle."

James did not respond.

"Aren't you going to say anything?"

"I don't think that information requires a response," James said.

"Why did you leave early tonight?" Molly asked.

"It was pretty clear that you had other plans," James replied.

"Well, I didn't," Molly lied. "I was waiting for you, and then I tried to find you, but you had left. I got all dressed up for you tonight, and you didn't even care."

"Don't try that with me," James countered. "You're dealing with someone who in his heyday could lie circles around you. Your folks might fall for that load of bull, but I know better. I've seen many young ladies all dressed up in their finest skank wear, and they're not looking for a hamburger and a Coke."

Molly's eyes flashed. "I hate you!" she said.

James remained silent until they arrived at the ER. "Do you want me to carry you inside?" he asked.

"Of course."

"Then apologize."

A long pause, then, "I'm sorry."

"You're going to have to do better than that. What are you sorry for?"

Another long pause, "Everything."

"You're going to have to do better than that too. Are you sorry that you lied to me?"

"Yes."

"Are you sorry that you were going to go out partying and get yourself into trouble?"

"Yes."

"Are you sorry that you said you hate me?"

An even longer pause, "Yes."

"Repeat after me. 'I do not hate James'."

"I do not hate James."

"That's a good start. Now say, 'I will not lie to James in the future.'"

"I will not lie to James in the future."

James got out of the truck and walked to the passenger's side. This time when he picked her up, Molly laid her head on his chest and closed her eyes.

Chapter 43

For the past month Molly had not been able to stop thinking about her father. When she knew that she would have another Saturday and Sunday as her days off, she called him and asked if she could meet with him.

"Don't tell Mom. I can't deal with her right now. I just want to see you," she had said during her phone conversation with him.

"Your timing's good," Boomer had replied. "Mom's going to Houston this weekend for the Christian Women's Council. She's leaving Thursday night and won't be back until Monday. She's one of the organizers and needs to get there early and stay until it's over."

"When can we meet?" Molly had asked.

"Where are you?"

"I'm in San Antonio. I came back in January."

Boomer was surprised to learn that Molly had returned to Texas but thought that it was better that he not say anything about it. He thought that Molly must be in some sort of trouble if she wanted to see him.

"Since you're so close to Austin, why don't you meet me at the lake house? I can get up there late Friday night. You come up early on Saturday and we can spend the weekend together."

"Okay," Molly replied. "I'll be there."

"Is there something that you want to tell me now?"

"No."

"Is something wrong?"

"No. I don't know why you always think something's wrong."

"Well then, I'll see you on Saturday. I love you."

"I love you too," Molly mumbled so reluctantly that her response was barely audible.

Boomer thought about Molly as he battled the weekend traffic on his drive to Austin on Friday evening. He felt certain that she would not have contacted him if she were not in some sort of trouble. He had prayed for her numerous times since she had called him on Wednesday afternoon, but he could not get past the cold fear that had dominated his waking moments since her call.

His imagination ran wild as he tried to imagine every possible scenario. Was she pregnant? Did she have AIDS? Was she in some sort of legal trouble? The more he allowed himself to think about the possibilities, the more distressed he became.

As he drove he prayed and asked Jesus to give him wisdom in dealing with Molly. "Oh, dear Lord, please help me to say the right things to bring her back to you. Please save her and help her to become the woman you created her to be."

By the time he had made the turn that led to the lake house Boomer felt a little calmer. He had promised himself that he was going to try to be led by the Holy Spirit to say and do the things that would witness best to Molly. He understood that nothing he had said or done since she had left to attend design school in San Francisco had made an impression on her, and he knew that without God's help he was not going to be able to make a difference this weekend.

Boomer had felt a little guilty about not telling Elizabeth about his meeting with Molly. He had not lied to Elizabeth; he had told her that he was going to the lake house to "check on things up there" while she was in Houston, but he had not told her anything about Molly. He reminded himself that not telling someone something is not lying. Elizabeth had not asked him what he was going to do at the lake house. Just the same, he felt ashamed that he had kept his meeting with Molly a secret.

On Saturday morning Boomer made a pot of coffee but did not eat. He knew that Molly would be restless when she arrived, and he thought that he could take her to The Herb Garden for lunch. Boomer would never have gone to The Herb Garden on his own. It was one of those chick places that women love because they serve food with sprouts and pomegranate seeds on top. He was an eggs and biscuits with chicken fried steak kind of guy, but he knew that Molly liked trendy restaurants, and this weekend was about her.

Molly arrived looking better than Boomer had expected. She was wearing skinny pants and a sweater with high-heeled boots. She looked rested and healthy although much too thin. It was 11:30, and Boomer was starving.

"Let's go get some lunch," Boomer suggested. "Are you hungry?"

"Not really. We can do whatever you want."

"Well, I'm famished! I have a restaurant picked out that I think you'll like. It's one of Mom's favorites."

The Herb Garden was only about fifteen minutes from the house, but they had a thirty-minute wait. During that time Molly said little, and Boomer struggled to think of topics that would not be "hot buttons."

Finally they were seated. Molly ordered coffee and an egg white omelet with feta cheese, sprouts, and sundried tomatoes.

"Can I get a BLT?" Boomer asked Tiffany, the college student who was waiting their table.

Tiffany rolled her eyes and pointed to the menu. "We have a cobb sandwich that is pretty much the same thing. It's bacon, tomato, avocado, and sprouts served on a croissant."

"I'll have that," Boomer replied. "Hold the sprouts, double the bacon, and add mayo."

"I don't think we can do that."

"Of course you can do that. Charge me for a side of bacon to make up for the extra on the sandwich, throw the sprouts in the garbage can, and slap a little mayo on the bread."

"I'll have to ask the manager."

"If he says, 'no', send him over here and I'll talk to him."

When the food arrived, Tiffany deposited the cobb sandwich in front of Boomer. A tiny container of mayo and a side of bacon accompanied it.

"Can I get you anything else?" she asked.

"I'd be afraid to ask for anything else," Boomer replied.

He took the top off his sandwich, removed as many sprouts as possible, added the side of paper thin strips of bacon, and spread the top slice of the croissant with mayo. The sandwich came with kale chips made fresh on the premises. Boomer popped one in his mouth, frowned, and pushed the rest aside.

Molly only picked at her omelet, but she devoured every crumb of the Dutch apple muffin that came with her meal.

Just as Boomer was beginning to relax, he heard a shrill voice from several tables away, "Boomer Anderson! What in the world are you doing here?"

He turned to see Betsy and Brad Collins grinning at him over plates of a disgusting-looking mixture of greens topped with dried cranberries and raspberry vinaigrette. Immediately, Betsy was on her feet charging toward their table. Boomer braced himself.

"Hey, Betsy," he said forcing a smile.

"What are you doing here without Elizabeth, you handsome devil?" Betsy was eyeing Molly suspiciously.

"Betsy, you remember my daughter Molly? Elizabeth went to Houston for the Christian Women's Council this weekend, and Molly and I thought we would come up and check on things at the lake house."

Betsy looked carefully at Molly and then seemed disappointed when she had confirmed that Boomer was, indeed, having lunch with his daughter rather than just someone young enough to be his daughter. "Are you visiting?" Betsy asked Molly.

"I'm working today. I'm a food critic," Molly replied pulling out her cell phone and photographing her omelet. "I'm only giving this place one star. Do you actually eat here often?"

Betsy was completely flustered by this new bit of information. "Tell Elizabeth I'll call her next week," she said to Boomer. "It was good to see you again, Molly."

Molly smiled and nodded as Betsy hurried back to Brad and the wilted pile of greens.

∞

When they were in the car headed back to the lake house, Boomer began to laugh. "The look on Betsy's face was priceless. She'll spend all weekend trying to figure out whether you actually are a food critic."

"No she won't," Molly replied. "She's convinced that I am, and now that she knows I gave her restaurant only one star, she'll never eat there again."

Suddenly, Boomer thought of something. "Do you remember when Mom and I used to take you and Tracy to Six Flags? You loved to ride the Merry-Go-Round; I'd always stand by you and Mom would stand by Tracy."

Molly felt her heart jump, and she quickly looked at her father.

"I haven't thought about that for years," Boomer continued. "You always insisted that I put you on the white horse with the pink saddle. You said it was yours, and no matter how hard I tried to explain that the horses belonged to the park, you were adamant."

Boomer reached over and took Molly's hand. It was cold, but it warmed quickly in his warm grip.

∞

That evening Molly sorted through the DVDs at the lake house and found a comedy that she had loved as a child. Boomer made an enormous bowl of buttered popcorn, and they settled down to enjoy their movie.

When the movie had ended, Molly appeared to be much more relaxed. Boomer knew that this would be his best chance of talking to Molly about getting her life on track.

"Molly, I love you, and I want you to have a good life," he began.

Immediately she interrupted him, "I want you to have a good life too."

"Thank you," Boomer continued, "I worry about you. You need to turn your life over to Jesus Christ. You know the truth, but you haven't lived in it for a long time."

Molly's eyes flashed. "I'm a Christian! I'm a much better Christian than most of the people in this family. I have a lot of faith, and I pray a lot!"

"That's good," Boomer replied. "You need to get into a good church and make some Christian friends."

"I am in a good church! I go to church all the time. Most of the time I think I'm the only one there who knows anything about the Bible. You know that I know my Bible!"

Boomer made a few more attempts to gently bring about a conversation on the state of Molly's soul, but she was so defensive that it was impossible to talk to her about her need to repent of her sinful lifestyle and to begin making better life choices. About midnight Boomer gave up and went to bed.

The next morning when Molly awakened, for a few seconds she did not know where she was. She thought that she was still a teenager and that she was at the lake house with her family. As she became fully awake she realized that many years had passed since she had slept in her Princess bedroom. She was surprised that her mom had not changed it.

When she asked Boomer about it at breakfast, he told her that Elizabeth had been adamant about keeping it exactly as it was when Molly was living at home. "She says that it is her link to you. Whenever we come up here she goes into your room and sits for a while. Did you look in the chest? The clothes you left in the chest the last time we all came up here are still there."

Molly did not answer, but Boomer saw her expression change. He could not tell whether she was touched, or sad, or pleased, but a fleeting trace of genuine emotion flickered in her eyes and danced around the corners of her mouth.

After breakfast Boomer and Molly left. When Boomer told her good-by, he held her in his arms for a long time. He wanted to keep her there forever, but he knew that until

Molly was ready to face the truth about her own life, nothing would change.

Boomer locked up and watched from the front porch as the little BMW sped down the winding road that led to the highway.

On Friday evening when Molly and James were settled in a booth with their burgers and fries, Molly decided that she would tease him a little.

"I guess the girl you marry will have to agree to become a Christian," she said in her most seductive manner.

"Heck no!" James responded. "I'd never marry a girl who became a Christian for me. The girl I marry will be a Christian because she loves Jesus more than anything. She'll know that Christianity has real, genuine, value, and if she were the only Christian left in the whole world, she'd stick with it because she knows that, in the end, it's the only thing that matters.

"Other things matter too," Molly responded. "Love, and family, and patriotism are important."

"There is no love apart from Jesus. If you don't know how to love Him, you don't know how to love anyone. Families are one of God's gifts to mankind, and patriotism must be tied to Christian principles or you may find yourself supporting another Third Reich."

"You don't think that people who aren't Christians love their children?"

"They love them as much as they are capable of love, but unselfish, sacrificial love comes from Jesus Christ."

"I'm going to start nursing school," Molly blurted out.

James looked surprised. She was glad that she had been able to catch him off-guard and gain some control over the conversation.

"What made you decide to do that?"

"Macy's been talking to me. She thinks I'd make a good nurse. I'm smarter than she is so I would be able to do it without any problem."

"What makes you think you're smarter than Macy?"

"Oh, come on! You're not serious!"

James ignored that. "Are you serious? About nursing school?"

"Yes, I've already applied to begin the summer semester."

"Here in San Antonio?"

"Of course. I've decided on UT San Antonio. Macy is helping me get a partial scholarship from the hospital. Later, I'll have to take out some student loans, but the scholarship will get me started. If I go summers, I can finish in three years."

"Good for you!" James exclaimed.

"James?"

"What?"

"Do you think you would ever consider marrying a girl like me?"

James looked thoughtful and did not answer right away.

"Oh, forget it! I was just pulling your chain," Molly said.

"No, I'll answer your question. To tell the truth, I haven't thought about much else since the first day I walked into your hospital room."

Chapter 44

The Sunday after Easter an East Indian Missionary was scheduled to speak during the morning services. The pastor had been talking about his visit for several weeks, but Molly was not looking forward to hearing him. Many of the native missionaries barely spoke English, and it was often difficult, and sometimes impossible, to follow what they were saying. She had looked around the sanctuary for someone wearing white pants and a long white jacket with a Nehru collar. When she was unable to spot anyone who fit her description, she thought that he might have cancelled.

Praise and worship had ended and James had joined her on her pew. She looked at his profile as he sat praying with eyes closed. Molly thought that he looked very handsome. His features were small—almost delicate—and he seemed younger than his twenty-eight years. He was the kind of guy that people tried to push around, but Molly knew from experience that he could be a lot harder to deal with than any of the "tough guys" she had known.

The pastor was introducing the speaker, and Molly turned her attention to the front of the church. Dr. Savio Chaturvedi smiled as he clipped the microphone to the lapel of his charcoal grey western style suit. He was a small man with wire rimmed glasses and thinning hair cut very short. His appearance and demeanor were more that of a successful businessman than a missionary.

"It is a privilege to be here among my fellow Christians in the American Church," he said in perfect lightly accented English. "Today I want to share my story with you, not because it is my story, but because it is a story that is being played out all over the world, in every country and among all races. It is the story of redemption that began 2000 years ago at the cross and continues to play out every day in the lives of those who are willing to be both hearers and doers of the Word.

"My story begins forty-five years ago in India. I was born into a family of Brahmin priests. The priests are the highest caste in India, and the Brahmin priests are the highest members of the priesthood. We are the 'protectors' of the people and as such are not required to do any work. However, many of us become doctors, teachers, or scholars because these professions carry with them the responsibility of protecting others.

"My family have been doctors for five generations, and my father was a highly respected physician in India. When I was five years old, he took our family to London to spend two years working in his specialty. He rented a large country house and hired a nanny to look after my brother and me. My brother was four years older than I so he was away at school every day. My mother spent most of her days among the women in the Indian community playing cards and doing whatever women of privilege do to fill their hours. Because I had no playmates, I spent my days exploring the big house and gardens.

"One day I saw a strange woman standing in the hallway outside my bedroom. She was wearing a long dress with an apron and a white lace cap on her head. She looked at me but did not speak. I felt frightened so I looked away, but when I turned my eyes back to where she had stood, she was gone. She had been standing at the end of the hall, and there was no place that she could have gone. I ran as fast as I could to find my nanny, and when I did, I told her what I had seen.

"My nanny said that I had seen the ghost that haunted the house, and she told me not to worry because she was a 'friendly' ghost. Yet, I did worry. My child's mind told me that this was not a good thing. When my father came home that night, I was already asleep, but two days later I found him alone in the library and told him about the ghost.

"My father was a man of great self-control. That was one of the few times that I ever saw him show emotion. He seemed to me to be very angry; his eyes flashed and he stood and began to pace back and forth across the room.

"Then he turned to me and said, 'You did not see a ghost! We are Brahmin priests. We cannot interact with spirits, and spirits cannot interact with us. A spirit cannot enter a house where we are. It is not possible! That is why in India the priests who are exorcists stay at our house when they visit our city. Everyone knows that a spirit cannot attach to a Brahmin. If a spirit attaches itself to an exorcist, it cannot do us any harm because it cannot enter our home or reveal itself to us. Look at me, Savio; never speak of this again; do you understand?'

"I mumbled, 'Yes, Father,' and I never again spoke to him about the ghost, but I continued to see her. For two years I watched her pass through the rooms, and sometimes I heard her laughter and the sound of her footsteps in the hallways.

"When we returned to India, I never again saw a spirit, but I always remembered that I had seen a spirit when I was in London. As I grew older this became a source of anxiety for me, not because I feared that the spirit would harm me but because I knew that as a Brahmin priest I was special, and part of being special was not being able to see or interact with spirits.

"In India I attended a prestigious Christian school where I perfected my English and received an excellent education. This was not a problem for a Hindu of the highest class because Hindus believe that all roads lead to god. My father had no fear that we would be indoctrinated by our Christian teachers because Hindus are taught that the whole world is Hindu—whether the world is willing to accept that or not. A Brahmin never argues with anyone about his religion, nor does he attempt to convert anyone to his way of thinking. The only thing that matters is that one is on a good path.

"I accepted all that I was taught concerning Hinduism and concerning my place as a Brahmin priest of the highest calling. Yet, always it was with me, the memory of having seen a spirit and having heard the sound of its laughter and even its footsteps in the hall. I knew that the spirit could see me too because sometimes she looked into my eyes and beckoned with her hand for me to draw near to her.

"I could not speak of my experience with the spirit to anyone, but my heart was constantly troubled, and as I grew older I found myself articulating my greatest fear, 'What if I am not special?' I could not, of course, speak these words to anyone, but they sounded constantly in my mind, 'What if I am not special?'

"When I left my home to go to the university, I tried to silence this fear. I told myself over and over, 'You are born to a family of Brahmin priests; you are a protector, you are the highest of the high; you are above all others; no spirit can touch you.'

"At the university I began to leave some of my Hindu teachings behind. I began eating meat—which is strictly forbidden. Hindus are taught that all living things are part of the same life force, whether a person or a dog or a cat or a cow, we are all one. Life is an illusion; we perceive that we are separate from animals and from other human beings, but we are all one and the perception that we are separate is an illusion. Yet, I felt little guilt about my indiscretion.

"When I returned home for visits, I adhered to the vegetarian diet, but when I was in Europe or the United States, I ate oysters, and steak and pork, and I took special pleasure in my self-indulgences. As I partook of these forbidden delights, I reminded myself, 'You are special. You are a Brahmin priest—the highest of the high; you are special.'

"Eventually I became an oncologist and practiced for a while at MD Anderson Hospital in Houston. I was very proud. My patients put their faith in me and believed that I was their only hope of being well again. They treated me almost as if I were a god. Every year I became more filled with pride, and finally I stopped doubting that I was truly special.

"Then one day an old man who owned a ranch near Midland came to the hospital. Mr. Emerson had been diagnosed with stage four lung cancer, and he was very ill. When I finished my examination, I knew that he could not live more than a few weeks, but I wanted to give him hope so I told him that we would begin a course of treatment immediately.

"He looked me straight in the eyes and said, 'The only way I'm going to get better is if the Lord Jesus Christ decides in His perfect wisdom to heal me. My wife and kids begged me to come here and find out if there's anything that you can do for me. You and I both know there isn't, and I'm not willing to spend the last few weeks of my life on this earth taking treatments that will make me feel sicker than I already do.

"'I'm sixty-seven years old. I've spent my life doing the work that I loved best. My kids are grown and my wife is set so that she won't ever have to worry about money after I'm gone. I've known Jesus for fifty years, and I know that going to be with Him is the best thing that can ever happen to me, so I'm content. If He chooses to heal me, I'll stay here a while longer and spend more time with my wife and kids, but if He chooses to take me, well, that's better yet.'

"I had never heard anyone talk like that, and I wasn't sure how to respond so I said, 'Positive thoughts are important. We have discovered that it does not matter what a man believes as long as he has positive thoughts that produce positive energy. Good Karma makes good health.'

"My patient shook his head and then said something that changed my life, 'Positive thoughts aren't worth a plug nickel. You can think positive thoughts every minute of every day, and they won't keep you out of hell. You can do good deeds until you're so spent that you can't put one foot in front of the other, and it won't earn you a ticket to heaven. You can take all your wealth and give it to the poor, and it won't buy you any credibility with Jesus.'

"'There's one God—Jehovah, the God of Abraham, Isaac, and Jacob. There's one way—Jesus Christ, His only begotten son, and there's one comforter, the Holy Spirit that God sent to earth to dwell in us. If you're counting on anything else to save you, you're on the wrong path.

"'The problem is that people get to thinking that they're special. They're the god of their own universe, and they don't need anything else. But that's not true. The only special one that's ever been born on this earth is Jesus Christ. He gave up everything to humble Himself and live among us—the lowliest of the lowly. He stepped off His throne for a little while so that we could be reconciled to Him, and if you're counting on anything else saving you, you're going to be in for a horrible shock when you leave this world and stand before Him.'

"I was so upset by Mr. Emerson's words that I left the examining room as soon as possible. He was a rancher who raised cattle to satisfy the appetites of meat-eating Americans. He never considered that the cows were part of the same life force as he. His views were narrow and unbending; he had no concept of the many roads leading to god; he did not understand Karma; he did not understand that those far wiser than he had come to these truths after much study. But I knew better; I was a Brahmin priest, a protector, and I was special.

"Mr. Emerson refused the normal therapies that we use to treat cancers such as his, and he left, but six weeks later a small package addressed to me arrived at the hospital. Inside was a worn Bible and a letter from Mr. Emerson's wife. The letter informed me that he had died a week earlier and that he had asked his wife to send his Bible to me after he was gone.

"I was astonished that this man who had met me only once would want to give me such a personal gift. I opened it to the first page, and written across it in Mr. Emerson's own hand was, 'For God so loved the world that He gave His only begotten son that whosoever believes on Him shall not perish, but have everlasting life. John 3:16'

"I was familiar with this verse from having attended Christian school when I was a child in India, but, for the first time, it spoke to me. I realized that I was the 'Whosoever' about whom the verse spoke. That evening when I was alone in my apartment I began to read the Bible that Mr. Emerson had sent to me. I did not intend to become a Christian, but I wanted to know what this book contained that would cause a man to say that he would prefer to die and go to Jesus than to live on earth as a wealthy landowner surrounded by a family who loved him—even if it were only an illusion.

"But there was something else that puzzled me. If I am Whosoever, I am like everyone else, because everyone is Whosoever. If I am like everyone else, I am not special. However, if God will come down from heaven and become a man to die a painful, humiliating death to save me, then I must be special. Even if I am like every other Whosoever, I am special. I am more special than a Brahmin priest because God died for me. I was very confused.

"After that I spent every evening reading the Bible and thinking about all that I had been taught at the Christian school when I was a child. One night as I sat reading I cried out, 'Jesus! If you are real, let me know. I am a Brahmin priest, and I cannot conduct myself like a common man and cling to a hope that will take me to a foolish place of bad Karma. If there exists anything that is not an illusion, I need to know what it is! If there is only one path, I need to know how to find it!' I cried out in this manner for some minutes, but only silence answered me. Then, just as I had decided that this reading of the Bible was nonsense that was unsettling my mind, my eyes caught sight of a verse on the page before me, 'I am the Way, the Truth, and the Life, and no man comes to the father except through me'.

"I cannot explain how I knew that this was the answer that I was seeking, but I knew. Everything that God had put into my life through my earliest childhood associations with Christians suddenly came together, and I knew that Jesus is the Way, and the Truth, and the Life, and I knew that I could come to God only though knowing Him.

"I spent the next years studying the Bible and attending church. Finally, I resigned my position at MD Anderson and enrolled in a Bible School. My heart's desire was to tell my people about Jesus Christ, and I committed my life to taking the truth to my people. After I graduated, I returned to India and began serving my people as a missionary."

Dr. Chaturvedi spent the remainder of the service talking about his missionary work in India, but Molly heard little of what he said.

Chapter 45

𝓘n mid-July Molly took her place in the circle of chairs in her CR group and listened to each member introduce herself to the group as they did every Friday evening:

"Hi, my name is Angela. I am a believer in Jesus Christ who struggles with drugs."

"Hi, my name is Christine. I am a believer in Jesus Christ who struggles with depression."

"Hi, my name is Linda. I am a believer in Jesus Christ who struggles with anger."

As Molly waited for her turn to come, she tried to think of a clever response. She had been attending for weeks, but she had never addressed the reason why she was there. She told herself that she was only in CR so that she could use her contacts there to ask for favors, and she had convinced herself that this was true. She could not bring herself to tell the group that she was struggling with anything, and her introduction was always the same, "My name is Molly, but you already know that." The group would then pause while they waited to see whether she would add anything to her introduction, and, when it was apparent that she had nothing further to say, they would go on to the next woman.

When her turn came, Molly replied, "My name is Molly, but you already know that." She had been unable to think of a witty tag and had lost yet another opportunity to shine in front of this group of losers.

As the session wore on, Molly made a decision not to return. She was not like these women. She did not have a need that could not be met by a few thousand dollars a month and a great apartment. There was no reason for her to continue to attend week after week while they poured out their deepest, darkest secrets and she counted the minutes until the sessions ended.

That night Molly waited for the other women to leave before she let Donna know that she would not be returning. She had actually looked forward to seeing the expression on Donnas' face when she gave her the news, but when the time came to tell her, Molly felt a sense of dread.

"Donna," she said, "I want you to know that this is my last night for CR."

Molly was disappointed that Donna did not appear to be surprised. "I'm sorry to hear that," she said smiling.

Molly wanted Donna to plead with her to remain in the group. "I might come back sometime," she said watching Donna carefully for her reaction.

"Well, you're always welcome," Donna replied.

Molly had never anticipated that Donna might be willing to simply allow her to walk away without questioning her reasons for leaving. "I don't belong here," Molly continued. "I'm not like these other women."

Donna continued to smile. "Whether you attend the group has to be your decision. If I can ever do anything for you, let me know. Good Luck!"

Donna had finished stacking the chairs against the wall and was moving toward the door. She stood outside and waited for Molly to pass through before turning out the lights and locking the room. Then, without another word, Donna walked down the hall and disappeared around the corner.

Molly was dumbstruck! How could her CR leader be so irresponsible? Donna Dawson was supposed to help the women in her group overcome their hurts, habits, and hang-ups, but when Molly had told her that she wasn't coming back, Donna had simply walked away without even asking why. Molly felt anger rise up hotly in her chest. She had suffered plenty—probably more than all of those other whiners put together, but Donna didn't care. The only thing she wanted was to have the women sit in that stupid circle and spill their guts so that they could all have a good cry, pray, and go home.

James was waiting for Molly at the front entrance, and he knew from the expression on her face that something was wrong.

"What's the matter?" he asked.

"Nothing!"

"Do you want to go eat?"

"No! I want a drink!"

"Like an iced tea or a Coke?"

"No. I want a real drink."

"Okay. I guess I'll be going on home. See you Sunday," James replied.

"What's the matter with having a drink!" Molly shouted. "Jesus drank wine, but you wouldn't know it from hanging around with you!"

"When you can walk on water and raise the dead, I'll reconsider whether I think it's okay for you to drink," James countered as he turned his back and walked away leaving Molly standing just outside the locked door.

"James! You come back here!" Molly shouted.

James turned and retraced his steps. "I'm going to tell you something. I love you. I've loved you since the day that I first walked into your hospital room. I want to marry you, but I can't deal with you. I'm not going to spend the rest of my life walking on egg shells so that I won't provoke a tantrum. I'm not going to be your whipping boy, and I'm not going to allow you to make my life hell on earth.

"When I met you, I thought that you just needed someone to help you get out of a bad situation. You had burned a lot of bridges with your family, and I could understand that because I did the same thing with mine. But I also thought that if I could be a real friend to you and help you understand that you can have a good life, it would make a difference. Apparently, I was wrong.

"From everything you've told me, I'd say that you have a great family who loves you and would do just about anything for you. I've done everything I know to do to help you get your life straightened out. Macy and Donna have been good friends to you. But no matter what anyone does, it's never enough for you. The truth is, you've got lots of people who love you, but you don't want to be loved. The only thing you want is to hang out with criminals because you think they're tough. When they beat you up and put you in the hospital, that just serves as further proof to you that they are tough.

"I'm through. If you ever decide that you're serious about changing your life, you know where to find me." James then turned on his heel and walked away.

On Saturday morning Molly went to the park to get her run in before it got too hot. She was dressed in very short hot pink running shorts and a matching top. She felt that she looked amazing, and she was certain that every male eye was on her as she ran around the perimeter of the park. When she had finished her run, she sat on a bench and dabbed her face with a small hand towel that she had brought with her. As she did so, she noticed a small man wearing Bermuda shorts and a polo shirt carrying a microphone. He was followed by a young guy in a baseball cap and baggy jeans carrying a video camera. Molly surmised that Bermuda shorts was taping a segment for the news, and she was certain that he would approach her.

Her long hair was pulled back in a ponytail, and, in order to make herself look more stylish, she removed her headband and wound it around the elastic band that secured her ponytail. She then sat still waiting for him to approach. Bermuda shorts was taking a long time with his interviews, and Molly soon became impatient. Wetting her lips, she rose from the bench and walked directly toward the camera.

The interview was ending just as she arrived. Being careful not to look at Bermuda shorts or the cameraman, Molly passed as close to them as possible without making contact. Just as she had anticipated, she heard a man's voice say, "Excuse me, Miss. May I ask you some questions."

Molly turned toward the sound of the voice and pretended to be surprised. She was certain that she was going to be on the evening news, and she couldn't wait for James to see her. It didn't matter how many other people they interviewed, she would make the cut. She had the ability to talk about subjects she knew nothing about and sound as if she had a genuine opinion. Besides, she was by far the best looking woman in the park. They weren't going to bump her for that fat mom pushing her bawling brat in the stroller.

"I guess so," she answered, flashing a toothy smile and gazing directly into the camera.

"We're here today to get people's opinions on how to handle social problems," Bermuda shorts began. "I want to ask you what you would do in various situations. Is that okay?"

"Yes," Molly responded as she continued to smile into the camera.

"Imagine that you are on a ship with five thousand passengers. The ship is going to sink unless one of the passengers is thrown overboard. The Captain comes to you and says that the other passengers have voted you the responsibility of choosing which passenger to throw overboard. Would you do it?"

Molly was surprised. This was not the question she had expected, but she liked the idea of this mind game, and she answered, "I would find out how many lifeboats we had and see if I could get enough people into lifeboats to save the ship," she replied smugly.

"There are no lifeboats," Bermuda shorts said. "Only one passenger needs to be thrown overboard so that the remaining four thousand nine hundred ninety-nine can live. If you refuse to choose one to be thrown overboard, everyone will die."

"That's hard," Molly responded. "But I guess I would. I mean it would be better to have one person die than to have everyone die."

"Now, imagine that you must choose among three specific passengers. The first is a frail elderly woman who is dying of a terminal disease; the second is a twenty-five-year-old soldier who has recently returned a hero from combat duty; the third is a two-month-old baby. Which would you choose to be thrown overboard?"

"I guess I would choose the old woman. I mean, she's going to die soon anyway, right?"

"Okay," Bermuda shorts said. "You would choose the old woman. Now the captain brings the old woman out on deck, and you discover that she is your grandmother. Is she still your choice to be thrown overboard?"

"Oh, that's really hard. I mean, it's hard, you know. I don't think I could have my grandmother thrown overboard. No. No. I wouldn't do it."

"Then who do you choose—the soldier or the baby?"

"I don't think I can do that. I would tell the Captain that I wouldn't do that."

"Okay, you tell the Captain that you are not willing to throw any of the three overboard, and he says that unless you choose one, he is going to have the crew throw you overboard. Are you willing to die so that the other passengers can live?"

"No! I'm not going to die for the other passengers. I don't even know them. I'm a good person and some of them are probably really bad. No!"

"Okay, so who do you choose?"

"I would choose the baby."

"Why the baby?"

"Because the baby wouldn't even know what was happening. It would die quickly and wouldn't even be afraid."

"What if the Captain told you that the baby was going to grow up to discover a vaccine that would eradicate cancer? If the vaccine is never discovered, when you are fifty-five years old, you will die a slow agonizing death from cancer. If the baby lives, you will be vaccinated, and you will never have cancer."

"You're making this too hard!" Molly exclaimed. "I choose the soldier."

"Now, let's imagine that you are on a different ship. This ship also has five thousand passengers, but each passenger is a convicted serial killer. They are en route to an island where they will be incarcerated for the rest of their lives. The Captain comes to you and says that unless you volunteer to be thrown overboard, the ship will go down and all of the passengers will die. Would you be willing to be thrown overboard?"

"No! Of course not! Why would I die for a bunch of murders? They deserve anything they get!"

"Do you know anyone who would be willing to die to save those five-thousand serial killers?"

"No. Everyone I know is too smart for that!"

"Yet Someone did die to save all of the serial killers, and all of the old women, and all of the soldiers, and all of the babies that the world has ever known. That one is Jesus Christ. He died for you and for me. He died for everyone, because in this world our sin has condemned us to death, and the only way that we can be saved was for someone who was Himself without sin to be willing to die in our place."

Molly was silent. Her bright smile had faded, and she felt tears well up in her eyes.

"Does this make you see things a little differently?" Bermuda shorts asked.

"Yes," Molly replied softly. "Yes. Yes, it does."

Chapter 46

The next few weeks were the busiest of Molly's life. Working at the hospital and attending her first semester of nursing school took up all her time. Molly had always been a good student, and she had thought that she would be able to breeze through her courses with little effort. She discovered, however, that she had a lot to learn. If she were going to do well, she would have to devote long hours to studying.

She had not returned to church, and James had not called. Macy was as friendly as ever when they saw each other at the hospital and acted as if nothing had happened, but she knew that Macy must be aware that she was not attending CR or Sunday services. She found it very annoying that no one had even tried to persuade her to return.

Molly had also begun having disturbing dreams. In one recurring dream she was in a phone booth trying to call her father. She started to punch his number into the phone, but half-way through, she would begin punching in the wrong numbers. When she tried again, she could not remember the number. When she awoke, she felt as if she had spent the entire night trying to make a phone call. In some of her dreams she found herself trying to get to class. She needed to dress, but she could not find her clothes. Hours and hours would pass with her trying desperately to get dressed so that she could leave for her class, and finally she would realize that it was already night, and she had never made it to school that day.

She decided that she would visit her parents over Labor Day weekend and called her mother to let her know that she was coming. Molly was not sure that her decision to visit them was a good one, but she had no friends and little money. As the time neared for her to go, she thought about backing out, but she felt that she could not deal with being alone for the holiday weekend.

The four-hour drive seemed to Molly to be much longer than it actually was. Miles of open spaces filled with flat land and hot blue skies did little to hold her interest. Her mind returned to Dr. Chaturvedi's testimony. He had turned to Christianity because he had discovered that he was not special. He seemed happy enough, but was he really happy? Was Christianity just a club for people who had managed to lose their specialness? Was it a last resort for people when they realized that their dreams were not going to come true? Did they embrace Christianity because they could use their "faith" as an excuse for their failure? They could pretend that their Christian convictions were all that was standing between them and success, and they could declare that they would be on top of the world if they had not chosen to willingly give it all up to follow Jesus.

Molly also thought about her interview with Bermuda shorts. At the end of the interview he had asked her to sign a waiver allowing him to use it as part of a Christian video. She had signed because she thought that there was a good chance that James and the rest of the congregation at the church would see it sometime. They would be blown away to see her in her pink running outfit answering Bermuda shorts' questions with the poise of a professional actress. But she was disturbed by certain aspects of the interview. She did not like being reminded that Jesus had died for her; it made her feel guilty.

As Molly entered the Dallas city limits, she suddenly felt very tired, but she was glad to be home. For the first time since she had left for San Francisco she would be able talk openly about her life. She could talk about nursing school and the church, and, under the right circumstances, she might even tell her parents about James.

For the first time in many years she prayed, "Dear God, please help me to get through these next few days."

That night Molly's nightmares returned. She could hear a little girl crying, "I want my mama! I want my mama!" The sound of that voice was so annoying that Molly wanted to tell the owner to be quiet, but while she was trying to think what to do, she awakened and realized that the she was the one crying for her mama. Elizabeth was sitting on the edge of her bed with her arms around her telling her that it was alright.

"Mama's here. You're okay. I won't let anything bad happen to you."

When Molly was fully awake, she was embarrassed. "I had a nightmare," she mumbled.

"Tell me about it," Elizabeth said as she continued to hold her daughter in her arms.

"I don't remember. I was lost. I was trying to find my way home, and I was scared."

"You are home, Sweetheart. You're safe. Go back to sleep."

∞

After church on Sunday Tracy and Marty came for dinner. They had been married for a little more than two years, but they still behaved like love-struck teenagers. Tracy was very attentive to her husband, and Marty looked at her as if she were the most wonderful woman on earth.

As Molly watched Marty she thought, "I've seen that look in someone else's eyes." She tried to remember where she had seen that particular love-sick expression, and then she realized that she had seen it in James' eyes when he had looked at her. Suddenly, she felt very much alone.

Molly talked about her church and her school. She told them how Macy had persuaded her to pursue a career in nursing, and she told them about Donna Dawson. She did not tell them that she had joined the CR group; she made it sound as if she knew Donna only through attending the church.

Finally, without intending to do it, she blurted out, "I met a guy!"

She had certainly not wanted to talk about James to Tracy and Marty, but watching them holding hands and acting as if they had something special that was exclusive to them was too much for Molly.

Both Elizabeth and Boomer immediately fixed their attention on Molly.

"Really? Tell us about him," Elizabeth said in her most upbeat manner, although, in truth, she was startled and feared that Molly had gotten involved with someone who would turn out to be bad news.

"His name is James. He's gorgeous. He goes to my church and plays guitar and sings in the praise and worship band."

Elizabeth's heart began to pound. She had prayed for Molly for so many years without seeing any results. Was God in this? Was Molly telling the truth? Did James even exist, or was Molly making him up to focus the attention on herself?

"What does he do?" Boomer asked.

"He works for a builder who also goes to my church. They build all sorts of stuff—luxury homes, commercial, you know."

"What does he do for the builder?" Boomer inquired.

"He's in charge of finishing and detail. You know, he makes sure that everything's perfect because they have like really high-end clients."

"What's the builder's name? I might know him," Boomer said.

"Ferguson Building Corporation. Billy Ferguson is the owner but he's at least ninety so he turned it over to his grandson Tracer who's James' best friend. James was already working there before Tracer took over, and they were already best friends, so he didn't get the job because of Tracer. Billy was the one who hired him."

"Billy Ferguson!" Boomer exclaimed. "I've known Billy for years, and he's nowhere near ninety. He's in his seventies at the most."

"Well, he looks like he's a hundred," Molly countered. "Anyway, Macy's Tracer's wife, and she's my best friend." When she spoke those last words, Molly realized for the first time that Macy actually was her friend; in fact, next to James she was her best friend.

"I think I might have met James," Boomer said. "Five years ago when I went to San Antonio to talk to Billy Ferguson about building the Texas Grand Hotel there, a kid who worked for him was my driver for the week. I'm almost sure that his name was James. I wish I could remember. Elizabeth, do you remember when you came down to spend the weekend with me, and I introduced you to him?"

Elizabeth looked thoughtful. "I remember going there for the weekend, but I don't remember meeting your driver."

Boomer continued, "Molly, when you get back, ask James if a guy named Boomer Anderson ever sent him a pair of handmade boots."

"You sent him boots?" Molly asked. "Why would you do that?"

"He admired mine, and I wanted to show my appreciation to him for putting up with me all week."

No more was said about James until Tracy and Marty had gone home. Then Elizabeth reopened the subject.

"Are you and James serious?" she asked.

"He loves me and wants to marry me. He told me so," Molly replied.

"What was your answer?'

"Nothing, yet."

"You don't want to marry him?"

"It's kind of complicated. He's like really, really Christian. I mean he won't even kiss a girl until he's married. He made a promise to God or something to remain celibate until he's married. I'm really Christian too, but I don't know."

"Do you love him?"

Molly had never considered whether she loved James. She had thought about how he felt about her and how she could use his feelings to her advantage, but she had never thought about her feelings for him. Now she realized that she cared a lot about James.

"I think so."

"You either love someone or you don't," Elizabeth responded. "If you don't love him, leave him alone so that he can find someone who does. If you do, don't keep him waiting or someone else may come along and snatch him up."

The thought that some other girl might "snatch James up" was repugnant. Although she did not admit it to her mother, Molly could not imagine her life without James. That night when she was in bed with the lights out, she whispered into the darkness, "I love you, James."

Chapter 47

On Friday evening Molly returned to CR. Donna smiled when she arrived but gave no indication that she was surprised to see her. Before the meeting began, Molly asked Donna if she could talk to her afterwards.

"Sure, Honey," Donna replied. "We can go for coffee if you want."

When it came Molly's turn to "introduce" herself to the group she said, "Hi, my name's Molly. I'm struggling with almost everything."

Although Molly did not share any of her personal problems with the rest of the group, for the first time since she had begun attending, she listened to the other women. She realized that they were dealing with many of the same issues that were making her life difficult but with one added factor; most of them had children that they were trying to support. Suddenly, her own problems did not seem as overwhelming.

After the meeting ended, Molly suggested that she and Donna go to Big Bob's Burgers for coffee. She chose Big

Bob's because that was the place where she and James had gone every Friday evening, and she hoped that he would be there.

"Let's go to McDonald's," Donna suggested. "It's only two blocks away, and they're open late."

Molly was disappointed, but she agreed. When she and Donna were settled in a booth with their drinks, Molly began: "I went to visit my parents last weekend."

"How'd it go?"

"Okay, I guess. My mom really gets on my nerves. She's always hovering over me, trying to control me. I wish she would leave me alone. Every time she sees me she starts the same old thing: 'The past is not important. You need to ask Jesus for forgiveness for anything you have done wrong and then start making better choices. You can't change the past so let go of it.' She really drives me crazy with that stuff."

"You don't think that's good advice?" Donna asked.

"I don't know. It's always the same old thing. She believes that if I will get saved and start living a Christian life, my life will suddenly become all sunshine and roses. I tell her that I am a Christian and I do live a Christian life, but she won't let it go.

"When I was growing up, my parents expected us to be perfect. They had all of these rules. We had to go to church. We had to make good grades. I was not even allowed to date until my Junior year in high school. No drinking, no smoking, no drugs, no profanity. Nobody can live like that, and I got away from them as soon as I graduated. When I went away to college, I never really went back.

"My dad wanted me to come into his architectural firm as an interior designer and to work with him until I married the son of one of his rich friends. Then I would have some snotty-nosed little brats and devote my life to taking care of them.

"All I ever heard from my parents was that I was so smart, and so beautiful, and so talented. I could do anything I wanted to do; I could be anything that I wanted to be. That's a lot of pressure to put on a kid."

"Molly," Donna responded, "From the day you first walked into CR I have thought that you are me twenty years ago. I knew how to use men, and I could get just about any man I wanted. I lived to party, and I broke all of the rules. Of course, the guys I was with were violent and abusive because I didn't value men who were gentle and kind—I thought they were saps. I liked my men dangerous, so I always went after the bad boys. I thought that I was safe with guys who were quick to use their fists and not averse to using a weapon if the occasion called for it. The problem was that they were also quick to use their fists on me whenever I irritated them.

"My family was very poor. We lived in Tennessee where my dad worked as an auto mechanic. He would come home at night tired and greasy and angry, and he would start drinking as soon as he came in the door. He and my mom fought all the time; and when he would start hitting her, I would get so scared that I would hide under the covers of my bed. Someone had put an old family Bible in my room, and whenever I felt brave enough, I would take it under the covers with me and look at the pictures. I loved the old Renaissance paintings of Jesus with the lambs and Jesus blessing the little children. I used to wish that Jesus would come and take me away where I would be safe.

"I did not have anyone that I could talk to, but when I was in the second grade I had a teacher who suspected that something was wrong at home. She saw how shy and afraid I was, and she tried to talk to me about my family, but I was scared that anything I said would get back to my dad so I wouldn't tell her anything. After that she didn't ask me any more questions, but whenever she saw that I was especially upset, Mrs. Walker would take me into the hall and wrap her arms around me and pray for me. Her prayers were so sweet that I knew they went straight to Jesus' ears. The only time I felt safe was when Mrs. Walker held me in her arms and prayed for me.

"One day my dad picked up my little sister—she must have been about four years old—and threw her against the wall. That scared my mother because she realized that if they went on the way they were, he was going to really hurt one of us. The next day she packed my sister and me up and moved us to Wisconsin where we lived with her parents.

"I was in the third grade when we moved to Wisconsin, and I felt different from the other kids. For one thing, I lived with my grandparents, and that set me apart because I was the only kid in school who did not have some kind of home. One day I invited a girl who was a little friendlier than the others to come over to my house after school to play. She replied, 'You don't have a house! You live with your grandma!' I felt my cheeks burn hot with embarrassment.

"I also had a heavy southern accent. For some reason, my classmates thought that a southern accent meant that I was stupid. They constantly teased me about it, and as a result, I became even quieter and more withdrawn.

"After a year or so my dad decided to come north to find work, and he stopped to see us when he passed through Wisconsin. I don't know why my mother agreed to let him come to the house, but she did, and they decided that they were going to get back together.

"As soon as they were back together my parents began fighting again. About two weeks after they were reunited, they had a terrible screaming, dish-throwing fight. Afterwards my father sat my mother down and told her that it was time for them to get saved. He said that if they didn't find God, one of them was going to end up dead.

"My dad was the first to commit his life to Christ, and my mom followed soon after. I have never seen anyone change the way my dad did. All he could talk about was Jesus. He read his Bible every day, and witnessed to everyone he met. Even his eyes changed; after he came to know Christ, they were a deeper shade of blue. He became as loving as he had been violent, and he was determined to tell the whole world about the saving power of Jesus Christ.

"Even though my father had changed, I never felt completely comfortable with him. There was always a little piece of me that remembered that violent person who could knock you clear across the room with one blow. I learned to respect him, and after a time, I believed he had changed, but I was never fully convinced that one day he would not revert to that violent man who had caused me so much anguish. God used that lingering fear of my father, and whenever he told me to sit down because he wanted to tell me about Jesus, I sat down and listened.

"By the time I was sixteen, I realized that boys would do just about anything for me, and I began to use my newly discovered power to manipulate them. I partied every weekend, and everywhere I went I was the center of attention.

"When I was seventeen, I discovered that I was pregnant. I didn't want to tell my parents, and I talked my boyfriend Joey into marrying me. It was an ill-fated marriage, and I don't think that it would have lasted, but I never got a chance to find out. When we had been married for three months, Joey died of a drug overdose.

"The following years were filled with drugs, alcohol, and sex. By the time I was twenty-five I had two little boys but not much else. That's when I met my husband Tom. He was a real party guy—handsome and popular with the ladies. His family had money so he was able to party large without worrying about how he was going to pay the bills.

"Tom and I lived together for a couple of years before we got married. I'm not really sure why we did it, but we finally went down to the Justice of the Peace and made it legal. It was funny; after we were married I started thinking that we needed to start living like normal people. I spent a lot of time thinking about all of those talks with my father—me sitting silently and him telling me about Jesus' love for me.

"It's a long story, but eventually I surrendered my life to Jesus and started attending church. I immediately got into CR and started working through my addictions, as well as my issues with low self-esteem. It took me another couple of years to bring Tom in, but eventually he started going to church with me and got involved in one of the CR groups for men.

"That was the beginning of a whole new life for me. I was clean and sober, and I had a Christian husband. I could do anything I chose with my life, and I chose to become a CR leader. I'm now a Ministry Leader and State Representative for Texas. I travel around the state helping churches set up their CR ministries, and I attend meetings in California, but my primary focus is CR in my home church. I've been a CR leader for fifteen years, but most mornings when I wake up I can hardly believe that God has been so good to me. I am happier than I ever believed it was possible to be, and I am more blessed than I could have imagined."

Molly had remained silent while Donna shared her testimony, but she thought that Donna was wrong. She and Donna were nothing alike. Molly had been raised by parents who had lavished affection on her. She had lived in a mansion in a fairy-tale setting, surrounded by gardens and fountains. She had traveled extensively and stayed in the most beautiful hotels and eaten in the trendiest restaurants. When she was living at home, her clothes were expensive and tasteful. Her prom dress had cost fifty-five hundred dollars. She could not imagine why Donna would say that the two of them were alike, but to say that Molly was Donna twenty years ago was downright insulting.

"During the past fifteen years, I've dealt with hundreds, maybe thousands, of young women," Donna continued. "One thing I've learned is that by the time they get to CR there are only two kinds:

"First, there are the ones like me who blame their dysfunctional lifestyles on having been poor and disadvantaged. They blame their parents for not caring what they did. They complain that no one thought that they were worth anything, and no one ever expected anything from them. They claim that they partied and drank and took drugs and had sex with strangers so that they would feel loved. They were just looking for acceptance.

"Then, there are the ones like you who blame their dysfunctional lifestyles on having parents who expected too much from them. They complain that their parents expected them to be perfect and always encouraged them in everything they ever did. One young woman told me, 'My parents expected me to start at the top and work my way up.' Apparently, she thought that she was being very clever, because every time she said that she paused to see whether I was properly impressed with her witty paraphrase. They excuse their own bad behavior by saying that they would not allow their parents to continue to control them, and they partied and drank and took drugs and had sex with strangers so that they could be free. The girls who were brought up in Christian homes blamed Christianity for their woes. They said that because they had to obey so many stupid rules they could never have cool friends, and that Christianity had kept them from being popular.

"The thing I have learned from fifteen years of dealing with girls in denial is that no matter where you come from, no matter what your background is like, no matter how well or poorly you have been taught, who you are comes down to one thing: You will become the person you choose to be. Girls who start the party cycle and all that it leads to end up alone. They are the victims of abuse from guys who learn to hate them. They are broke and, more often than not, diseased. They come from many different places, but they all end up in the same place. They get there by deliberately choosing sin and rebellion and then excusing their own bad behavior by saying that it was all their parents' fault.

"That's why I said at the beginning that you and I are just alike," Donna continued. "We were two beautiful young women from opposite sides of the track, but we ended up in the same stink hole because of our own bad choices."

Molly felt that she had been stripped bare of all her excuses, and she did not know how to respond. She thanked Donna for agreeing to meet with her and left as quickly as she could. As she drove to her apartment, hot tears rolled down her cheeks forming black rivulets of melted mascara that dripped onto her white tank top in wet gray blobs.

Chapter 48

Molly slept poorly, and at 6:00 on Saturday morning she called James. When he answered the phone, she knew from his voice that she had awakened him.

Without apologizing, she said, "I want to talk to you."

"Okay, How about breakfast?"

"Sure. Where do you want to meet?"

"The Country Kitchen at 7:30?"

"That's fine."

"Molly, are you alright?"

"I'm fine. I just want to talk to you."

When James arrived at The Country Kitchen, Molly was already seated in a booth drinking coffee. He took a seat opposite her and looked at her across the table. She was wearing an aqua blouse that brought out the color in her eyes, and James thought, once again, that she was the most beautiful girl he had ever seen.

"Where were you last night?" Molly demanded.

"What do you mean?" James replied. "I was leading my CR group, just like I do every Friday night."

"You didn't wait for me afterwards," Molly pouted.

"Why would I wait for you? You haven't been to CR for two months."

"James, you're so mean," Molly said in her most flirtatious manner.

"Why are we here?" James asked.

"I just need to talk," she answered much more seriously. "I went to see my parents last weekend."

"Was it a good visit?"

"I guess. My sister and her snobby husband were there slobbering all over each other. After they left, it was okay."

"I want to ask you about your family," Molly continued. "Did they constantly try to force you to be perfect?"

James was surprised at Molly's question, and he took a sip of his coffee before he answered. "Actually, my parents never tried to force me to do anything. Looking back, I realize that I was always a pain. I griped and complained about everything—especially going to church. I made such a big deal out of hating church that when I was fourteen my dad told me that I didn't have to go anymore. I never set foot in a church again until I came here."

"But still," Molly persisted, "they were probably always on your back about something."

"No. They had the idea that all kids go through a wild stage, but eventually they end up alright. No matter what I did, they just sort of took it in stride and waited for me to grow out of it. I knew that they loved me and that they were there for me. Being a stupid kid, I didn't appreciate them, but my biggest complaint about them was that they weren't cool. I didn't understand how two boring people like them could have a son as cool as me.

"My dad was a high school algebra teacher until he retired a couple of years ago, and my mother was a stay-at-home mom. I never saw my parents fight, and I never came home from school to an empty house. My mom is a great cook; she makes the best Italian food in the world, and we always had big dinners. We never had a lot, but we weren't poor. They still live in the same house that they bought when I was in kindergarten. They went to the Methodist church every Sunday; they paid their taxes and were good neighbors. If you look up the word 'normal' in the dictionary, you'll see both their pictures next to it.

"After I gave my life to Jesus, I went to see them and paid back some money that I owed them. I told them about my new relationship with Christ, but they weren't very open to it. They had been in church all of their lives, and they thought that they were saved. I don't know; maybe they were, but they didn't have a personal relationship with Jesus, and I wanted that for them.

"It took a couple of years and a lot of visits before they really committed their lives to Christ. My dad came in first. He said that my paying back the money was what convinced him. He knew when I handed him the check that I had changed, but it took him a while to come to the conclusion that he needed a deeper walk with Jesus himself. My mom made a commitment a few weeks later.

"Now my brother and sister have also accepted Christ. They are living for Jesus and teaching their kids to do the same. It took longer than I thought it would, but my whole family is now serving Christ."

Molly changed tactics, "You've never told me how you ended up in CR."

"And I never will. The James who joined CR died the night that he accepted Jesus. We buried him in the water of the baptismal of San Antonio Believers Church. I was born that night when I rose from that watery grave, and I have refused to look back. Lots of people seem to enjoy talking about their old lives before they accepted Jesus, but I'm not willing to exhume the old James and wipe the cobwebs out of his eyes so that I can parade him around and talk about his sins."

Molly was unprepared for James response. "Well," she said, still attempting to turn the conversation to her advantage, "My mom was doing what she always does. She started telling me that everybody makes mistakes, and everybody does things that they wish they could go back and change, but that's not possible. When we realize that we are on the wrong track, we need to stop, ask God to forgive us, and immediately start making better choices. She says that God doesn't care about the past. The only thing that is important is to accept His forgiveness and move forward.

"I don't know why she always gives me this same speech. Every time she starts I tell her that I am a great Christian. I know my Bible, and I pray. I'm a better Christian than she is, but no matter what I say she just keeps on telling me that I have to turn my life around."

"What part of that speech has you confused?" James asked.

"All of it! Why does she keep telling me that same thing over and over?"

"Molly, what your mother is telling you is the very heart of the gospel. Until you will admit that you are a sinner and ask Jesus to forgive you, your life will never change. The beauty of Grace is that Jesus' death on the cross made it possible for us to be forgiven for our sins, but we are more than forgiven; our sins are actually washed away! They're gone! As if they had never happened! But you can't be forgiven until you will admit that you are in need of forgiveness. The next step is to start making better choices. You have to make a commitment to live for Jesus and get the things out of your life that separate you from Him. This isn't rocket science! If it were, only a few guys at NASA would ever get saved."

By the time James had finished speaking Molly knew that she had come to a place where she had to make a decision that would impact the rest of her life. She could walk out of The Country Kitchen, get into her car and head back to California, or she could give her life to Christ and turn loose of everything that made her special.

Chapter 49

Molly reached over and took James' hand in hers. They were in his truck headed toward her parents' house. The sun was shining; the sky was clear; everything was perfect. Molly looked at James and smiled. She was happier than she had ever been in her life.

When she had surrendered her life to Christ and accepted Jesus not only as her savior, but as the Lord of her life, everything had changed. Molly had never been able to do anything half-way. When she had rejected Christ, she had sinned to the fullest; when she had repented, she had become a full-time evangelist. Whether she was at school or working at the hospital, she told everyone she met that they needed Jesus.

"I just remembered something," she said. "My dad told me to ask you whether Boomer Anderson ever gave you a pair of handmade boots."

James started visibly. "Oh, my gosh! Is Boomer Anderson your father? I never put it together."

"Did he give you some boots?"

"Yeah, he sure did!"

James had turned very pale. "What's the matter?" Molly asked. "You look awful."

"I just don't know how this could have happened. I mean, Boomer Anderson being your dad and all."

"Do you two hate each other or something?" Molly demanded. "You act like I just told you my father was Hitler."

"No. It's nothing like that. Your dad came to San Antonio to meet with Billy when we built the San Antonio Texas Grand Hotel. Billy had me drive him around for the whole week. He treated me great. I picked him up every morning, and he insisted that we have breakfast and lunch together. He paid for everything; I never ate so much in my life. Even though I was just a house painter and he was a rich guy, he talked and asked me about myself. He treated me like an equal.

"But, your dad's pretty intimidating. I was always nervous when he was around. He seemed to have everything—looks, money, education, position. I kept thinking that I was going to mess up, and when I did, he would think that I was a loser and tell Billy to get rid of me."

"Did he do that?"

"No! He was always really nice. He even introduced me to your mom when she came down for the weekend. By the way, you've got a good-looking mom."

Molly wrinkled her nose. "Well, there's nothing to worry about. My dad will be fine."

"What if he says that you can't marry me?"

"He won't."

"What makes you so sure?"

"I know my dad. He's different than you think. He's worked all his life, and he can't stand snobs. You two will get along great!"

James wasn't convinced, and by the time he stopped his truck in front of the Anderson residence he was literally shaking inside. It wasn't a house; it was a mansion. After working for Billy for almost ten years, James knew the value of luxury homes. Even in a low-cost housing market like Dallas, this one was worth several million dollars.

Molly was holding his hand and leading him to the front door. She reached out to open it, but before she succeeded, it flew open and there stood Boomer grinning from ear to ear. He threw open his arms and embraced them both at once.

"James!" he shouted. "I knew it was you the minute Molly told me about you, and I've been waiting to see you again ever since!"

James was astonished. Boomer had done it again! How could he stand there in that gorgeous house looking like a character out of *Giant* and appear to be unaware of any of the differences between them?

"Come in!" Boomer continued. "I hope you're hungry because Elizabeth has fixed enough food for an army, and that's just the appetizers! Elizabeth!" Boomer called loudly.

"I'm right here," came a small voice from behind him. Elizabeth stepped out from around her husband, gave Molly a quick kiss and extended her hand to James. "I'm Elizabeth, Molly's mother. We are so glad to have you here."

Elizabeth had wanted to keep this first meeting informal and had set up the appetizers and lemonade near the pool. James was relieved to see that it was food that he could identify—shrimp, spinach dip, chicken wings—real food.

A soft April breeze was barely perceptible as it stirred the air and carried with it the scents of clean pool water and flowers blooming in the garden. James began to relax, and as he ate the food and sipped a cherry Coke, he, too, began to forget about the differences between Boomer and him.

The next morning James woke early and walked out into the yard for some prayer time. He spotted the gazebo and started toward it. He had thought that everyone was still asleep, but as he drew closer he saw that Elizabeth was sitting on the padded bench that was built around the interior reading her Bible. He was about to retreat when she spotted him.

"James," she called. "Come up here and talk to me."

"I'm sorry," James responded. "I thought that I was alone. I didn't mean to interrupt you."

"You're not interrupting," Elizabeth replied. "This is where I read my Bible and pray whenever the weather is good. I'm glad you're here. Tell me about yourself."

James didn't know how to begin. He and Molly had come to her parents' home to tell them that they were going to be married, but they hadn't made the announcement last night. He had been caught off guard when he realized that Boomer was Molly's father, and he had not been able to get past the idea that he might not be welcome as a future son-in-law.

"There's not a lot to tell," James began. "I'm a CR leader at San Antonio Believers Church, and I sing and play guitar in the praise and worship band. Do you know what CR is, Mrs. Anderson?"

Elizabeth nodded, "We have CR at our church."

James continued, "I work at Ferguson Construction as their finishing and detail man. I started going to the church at the same time I started at Ferguson Construction. This makes nine years."

"How long have you been a Christian?" Elizabeth inquired.

"I got saved a few months after I started going to the church." James hoped that Elizabeth wouldn't ask too many questions. He was prepared to tell her and Boomer enough so that they would know that he had made some mistakes, but he did not want to drag up his past, and he hoped that they would not insist.

"Are you from San Antonio?"

"No Ma'am. My folks live in Ft. Worth."

"Why did you go to San Antonio?"

James thought carefully before he answered. He wanted to be completely honest, but he did not want to say more than necessary. "Ten years ago I was in a bad accident, and I almost died. I was leaving my parents house in Ft. Worth to return to Angel Fire, New Mexico, where I was living at the time. I wanted to get an early start and ride straight through so I left while it was still dark. I was sitting at a red light at an intersection in Ft. Worth when a pick-up truck came up behind me really fast. I heard it coming, but I didn't have time to move. It hit me and threw me about fifty feet onto a median...."

The color had drained from Elizabeth's face, and her heart was pounding. "What was the date?"

"May 5, 2011. I'll never forget it; in fact, I have my ten year anniversary coming up next month."

"You stay here. Don't move. I'll be right back." Elizabeth's body was shaking so violently that it caused her voice to shake too. Even though it was a warm day, she felt icy cold, and she wrapped her arms tightly around her as she ran toward the house.

James could not imagine what he had said to upset her, but it was evident that she was about ready to have a meltdown. He was sure that she would return shortly with Boomer in tow and that they would order him off their property and tell him never to contact their daughter again. Stunned, James reviewed everything that he had said, but he could not think of anything that would have caused such a reaction.

Soon James heard the sound of footsteps running on the path leading to the gazebo. He looked up to see Elizabeth running toward him. She was holding something close to her chest that looked like some sort of books.

When she arrived at the gazebo, she took the books in both hands and offered them to James. "Open volume one," she said, "and read the first three pages."

James looked at the notebooks and then opened the one titled, *The Timothy Diary, Volume One* and began to read.

"Friday, May 5, 2011. I woke up around 5:00 this morning from a strange dream."

James was stunned to discover that the notebook contained a detailed account of his accident. As he read further, he discovered that Elizabeth had determined almost immediately that what she had seen in her dream had really happened and that God had given her a vision of the events so that she could pray for him. She had written about his being her "spiritual son," and she had included her prayer that one day God would allow her meet him.

Now it was James' turn to weep. As he read, the tears streamed down his face, and his chest began to heave as great, loud sobs came from his throat.

As the two of them sat in the gazebo sobbing uncontrollably, Boomer appeared on the path. Alarmed at what he heard, Boomer rushed to the gazebo, looked at each of them and shouted, "Elizabeth! What did you do to James!"

Elizabeth attempted to answer, but when she tried to speak, the only sound that came out was a grainy squeak. James was beyond even making an effort at speech. He simply put his hand in the air and shook his head as if to say, "Stop!"

Boomer took a seat next to Elizabeth and waited until she was finally able to form a sentence, "Do you remember when I had that dream about the young man who was in a motorcycle accident, and I went to my prayer group to have the women pray for him?"

"No," Boomer replied.

"I named him Timothy. I've been praying for him for ten years."

"Oh, yeah, I know about Timothy. Are you two crying about Timothy?"

"This," Elizabeth said, extending her hand toward James, "is Timothy."

"Well, I'll be darned!" Boomer exclaimed. "Here I was all these years thinking you had a screw loose!"

"I have a lot of screws loose," Elizabeth responded, "but not about Timothy."

When she said that, she and Boomer both began laughing, and as Elizabeth laughed, the tears began to flow again until she was laughing uncontrollably with the tears streaming down her face.

After what seemed like a long time Elizabeth and James both gained control of themselves, and the three of them walked back to the house together. Before they reached the French doors that led to the kitchen, James asked, "Can I read these while I'm here?"

"Yes, of course."

When they entered the kitchen, Molly was sitting at the island drinking a cup of the coffee that Boomer had put on to brew before he had gone to look for Elizabeth. She was startled to see that both her mother and James had obviously been crying.

"I'm going to marry James no matter what you say!" she shouted.

"Hush!" Boomer returned.

Alarmed, Molly sat silently staring at James and her parents.

∞

When they were settled around the kitchen table with mugs of steaming coffee and a platter of Krispy Kremes, James spoke, "Molly and I came here to tell you that we plan to be married. However, I think she has pretty much already made that announcement. Just before we arrived I found out that Boomer Anderson was her father, and that nearly scared me to death. This morning Mrs. Anderson handed me three notebooks that apparently record everything I've done for the past ten years. I keep hoping that I'm going to wake up, but I don't think that's going to happen."

"I'm sorry that I didn't handle this better," Elizabeth said.

"No, Ma'am. Don't apologize. I owe you more than I can ever repay, and I want to tell you everything that has happened to me since my accident. I have never shared my full testimony with anyone because I don't think that it's very helpful to drag up all of the sin in my life and put it on display like it was something to be proud of. I've been forgiven for a long time, and I don't allow myself to relive my past. But this time I'm going to make an exception."

For the next several hours James told Molly, Elizabeth, and Boomer everything. He told them about going to California and getting on drugs. He talked about the accident and talking his father into getting him the marijuana. He told them how he had cheated his own dad by charging him much more than the street value and pocketing the money for himself. He told them about seeing Grady handcuffed in the front yard of their house in Angel Fire and about plotting his suicide by drowning himself in the Atlantic Ocean. He told

them about Billy and Tracer and Macy. He told them about
the church and his involvement in CR. At times he felt that
he was saying too much, but once he had started, he could
not seem to stop himself.

Elizabeth was not sobbing now, but as he talked the tears
streamed down her face. James was confirming everything
that the Lord had shown her concerning him, and she could
hardly take it in.

When James had finished telling his story, he reached
over and took Molly's hand. "I love Molly," he said. "She's the
only woman I've ever loved. I want you to know that I have
respected her and treated her like a sister in Christ. I've
never even kissed her, but I want to marry her more than I've
ever wanted anything. I understand if you can't give us your
blessing; I didn't intend to tell you about my past. I hadn't
even told Molly, but, considering the circumstances, I
thought you had a right to know."

Boomer waited for Elizabeth to speak, but when she
remained silent, he said, "I've given a pair of handmade
boots to only two people in my life. One was my father; you
know who the other one was. I'm thinking that since you got
my boots, you probably should have my daughter too."

"Dad!" Molly exclaimed, "That doesn't make any sense."

Finally Elizabeth spoke, "I've called you my spiritual son
for ten years. I've loved you and prayed for you and trusted
God that one day I would meet you. I think it's only fitting
that you should also be my flesh and blood son-in-law."

James spent the rest of the day sitting on the wide front
porch with the ceiling fans turning lazily overhead as he read
the diaries. It was all there. Although Elizabeth had not

known any of the details, the dates that she had felt led to have special prayer for him lined up with the times that he had gone through critical situations: his arrest, his hearing before Judge Chavez, even the day that he had gone to the hospital to talk to Molly. Elizabeth had noted next to that date that she felt something important was happening in his life, and she had prayed that he would be wise and strong and make good decisions.

By the time James finished reading, the shadows were long and the sun had taken on a golden late afternoon glow that peeked through the trees and cast its soft light across the grass. He closed his eyes and whispered, "Thank you, Jesus, for having pity on me and delivering me from sin and death into a life more beautiful than I could have ever imagined existed."

Chapter 50

Six weeks later the white garden was in full bloom. Pots of creamy roses had been placed around the base of the gazebo, and the soft white chiffon draperies that had been strung between its columns stirred in the gentle breeze. Molly and James had wanted a simple, informal wedding, and Elizabeth had done everything she could to ensure that they would get exactly what they wanted.

The guests had already arrived and were seated in the chairs that had been arranged on the lawn facing the gazebo—fifty three in all: James' parents, his sister and brother and their spouses and children, Molly's two sets of grandparents, Tracy and Marty, Macy, Tracer, and Billy Ferguson, Donna Dawson, the members of the praise and worship team, Tony Manzo and his wife, and a few other friends from church.

Rosie was not quite three years old, but she was excited about being a flower girl. Macy had spent hours rehearsing with her so that she knew exactly what to do. As she walked down the long strip of carpet that had been laid on the grass to form an aisle, she beamed with pride. Her golden red curls bounced as she carefully sprinkled the carpet with white rose petals. Everything in the wedding was white except Rosie's dress. She wore pale pink chiffon and a wreath of tiny pink roses atop her head. As she passed the guests with her shining green eyes and dimpled smile, whispers of, "How adorable!" "She looks like a little angel." "Ohhhh, how sweet!" floated through the air.

The strains of *The Wedding March* filled the garden through unseen speakers placed among the foliage, and Molly and Boomer began their walk down the aisle. Molly's simple white strapless gown, and her cascade of soft blonde curls reaching almost to her waist gave her a fairy princess appearance.

As Elizabeth watched them make their way to the gazebo, she experienced complete peace. There were no tears; she had spent ten years crying for Molly; today she had nothing more to cry about. God had answered her prayers. She had prayed for this day, and hoped for this day, and even believed for this day, but now that it was here, she could hardly believe that it was happening.

Elizabeth's attention turned to James. He was standing in the gazebo waiting for his bride. In his white tuxedo he looked every bit the part of Prince Charming. Boomer had always wanted a son, but Elizabeth had been completely satisfied with her two daughters. She thought it was ironic that God had given her a spiritual son who would now forever be a part of her life—a real life flesh and blood son. She could see from the expression on his face how much he loved Molly, and once again she breathed a prayer of thanks for all that God had done for her and her family.

Chapter 51

The years that followed were the happiest of Elizabeth's life. Her girls gave her five beautiful grandchildren. Molly had twin boys—Travis and Bowie. Tracy gave birth to Bradley Charles, whom everyone called Brad, the same year that Molly had the twins. Later Tracy had two girls, Sarah Elizabeth and Melanie Ann. The three boys were inseparable, and the family often remarked that they were more like triplets than cousins.

James and Marty became instant friends. In spite of Marty's privileged upbringing and James' middle-class background, the two men found that they had much in common. They shared an interest in architecture and construction, and they both loved the Lord with all their hearts.

Soon after Molly finished nursing school, she and James agreed that he should attend seminary while she worked. James enrolled in a seminary in Dallas, Molly found a job with a hospital there, and they made the move. Boomer was thrilled that they were "coming home", and he hired James to work part-time while he attended seminary. Boomer soon discovered that Billy Ferguson had been correct when he had pronounced James to be "the best finishing and detail man I have ever seen."

Their husbands' friendship brought Tracy and Molly together much more quickly than they might have been reunited under other circumstances, and Molly apologized for the cruel things she had done to Tracy when they were teens. Tracy knew that the apology was sincere, and she chose to remember the relationship they had enjoyed when they were children and had loved each other. The girls promised that they would not discuss past hurts again, and they were able to become spiritual sisters as well as biological sisters.

Everyone, including James' and Marty's parents, got together to celebrate major holidays and the grandchildren's birthdays. Elizabeth loved entertaining her large family, and she often said that every hour spent preparing food and decorations was a blessing.

Everyone agreed that their favorite place for these get-togethers was the lake house in Austin. They tried to always meet there for Easter and Fourth of July when the wild roses were in bloom spreading their pink perfume across the field, and Molly always picked a basket full to float in the shallow cream-colored bowl that she had loved as a child.

Elizabeth constantly thanked God for having given her such a beautiful life. During the years when Molly had walked away from her faith, it had often seemed to Elizabeth that her prayers were in vain and that Molly would never come back. But she now knew that God had heard every prayer and seen every tear. She knew that He had moved in Molly's life to squeeze her, and put pressure on her, and bring her to the right place with the right people so that she would be saved and become the woman that He had created her to be.

Spring was Elizabeth's favorite time of year, and this was the most gorgeous spring day that she had ever seen. She was walking through the field behind their lake house in Austin, and even though she and her girls had walked in that field many times before, she saw it as if for the first time. The blue bonnets were in full bloom, and their beauty was accentuated by various other wild flowers in shades of red, yellow, and purple. The wild roses tumbled over the fence spreading into a cloud of pink that filled the field with their sweet fragrance. The soft warm air caressed her body bringing with it a feeling of total peace. As she continued through the field, Elizabeth was filled with a sense of joy and well-being that she had never experienced before. Then she spotted Him in the distance. It was Jesus smiling with His hand stretched toward her.

"This is what heaven feels like," she thought.

As she drew closer, her joy increased. "I never want to leave here."

Jesus was now standing directly in front of her, and she placed her hand in His.

The display on the clock on Elizabeth's bedside table read, "5:03 A.M., Friday, May 5, 2041."

∞

On Monday morning James walked to the front of Dallas Calvary Chapel where he had been the senior pastor for nine years. He was dressed in a dark suit and tie and a white shirt. He looked solemn as he addressed the crowd that filled the sanctuary.

"Today we celebrate the life of Elizabeth Anderson. Some knew her as a loving mother and grandmother; others knew her as a loyal friend. She was a quiet woman who loved people and treated everyone she met with respect. Whether a person had much or little made no difference to her. She recognized that everyone needs a relationship with Jesus Christ, and she spent her life helping others find that love of Jesus that brought meaning to their lives."

James wiped his eyes with his handkerchief and cleared his throat before continuing, "I thought that I knew Elizabeth well. I met her twenty-years ago, but Elizabeth met me long before that. Most of you have heard my testimony about how Elizabeth saw my motorcycle accident in a dream and prayed for me for ten years before she was finally able to verify that I actually existed. But there are many stories about Elizabeth that no one knew while she was alive.

"After we found her last Friday morning, Molly and I spent the weekend going through her personal effects. In doing so I discovered an Elizabeth I never knew. She had twenty-six notebooks filled with information about the people whose lives she touched and the circumstances under which she had met each of them. She never used last names so that the identities of everyone she wrote about in her diaries were protected, but she gave detailed accounts of her prayers for each of them. What is remarkable is that she did so much for so many, but she never talked about her work.

What she did, she did for Jesus, and He alone knows the extent to which she helped others.

"I discovered that when the girls were teenagers she began asking God to lead her to people who needed her help, and she was soon asking Boomer for money to invest in meeting those people's needs. Finally, in desperation, Boomer told her that he trusted her to make good decisions about how to best help those people God sent to her. He set up a bank account solely for that purpose and deposited four thousand dollars each month for her to spend on her ministry.

"Over the years Elizabeth bought shoes, coats, and blankets for thousands of children in the Dallas area. She often made dozens of sandwiches that she gave out to the homeless people who refused to go into the shelters. During cold weather, the sandwiches were usually accompanied by a blanket. But whether a person was the recipient of food, blankets, or clothing, if he received a gift from Elizabeth, that gift was always accompanied by a new Bible. Elizabeth ordered them by the case and kept several boxes in the trunk of her car at all times.

"In 2005 Elizabeth spent three weeks caring for two preschool children while their mother stayed at the hospital with their critically ill brother, John. On those days she not only cared for the children, she did the laundry, cleaned the house, and cooked the meals. When the mother returned from the hospital every evening, she found a meal prepared for her and her children safely asleep in their beds. On the day that John was released from the hospital, Elizabeth stocked the cupboards with food, put a stack of new towels in the bathroom, and made up all the beds with new sheets and blankets that she had bought for the occasion.

"Elizabeth wrote in her notebooks about her love for Boomer and her gratitude for his kindness and generosity. She and Boomer loved each other for more than fifty years, and when he died last year, Elizabeth missed him very much. Even in her grief, however, she told us that she knew that Boomer was with Jesus and that one day they would be together again.

"Boomer never really understood his Lizzie but he loved her and supported her in everything she did. He was a godly man who was widely respected for his honesty and integrity, and he appreciated the value of a Christian wife. Today we can rejoice knowing that he and his Lizzie have been reunited.

"Elizabeth led hundreds of people to Jesus, and that was her greatest joy. She was a true Crusader, but she got people's attention by being sensitive to their needs. King David was known in Israel as a great soldier, but he never fought more valiantly than Elizabeth.

"Unlike King David, however, Elizabeth did not fight with the traditional weapons of war. She armed herself with Truth, Faith, and Salvation, and she carried with her the Sword of the Spirit—which is the word of God. Her battles were not fought for land, or riches, or power. Elizabeth fought her battles for the souls of men and women, and whenever possible, she brought everyone with whom she came in contact to the Cross and led them to know Christ as their Savior.

"Elizabeth's most powerful weapon was prayer. Her notebooks attest to years spent in prayer for all those she led to Christ and for all those to whom she witnessed but who never accepted Him. The latter she committed to Jesus believing that He would send someone else to reap the harvest from the seed that she had planted. She was often tired and sometimes discouraged, but she never gave up.

"Elizabeth was a true Warrior—a Warrior in prayer, a Warrior in faith, and a Warrior in service. I am honored that Jesus Christ gave her the faith to spend a lifetime praying for a young druggie whom most people did not think worth giving a second thought. It is because of her faithfulness that I am here today and that I can proclaim Jesus with everything that is within me. It is with deepest gratitude and love that I say, 'Thank you, my faithful friend.'"

For we wrestle not against flesh and blood, but against principalities, against powers, against the rulers of the darkness of this world, against spiritual wickedness in high places. Wherefore take unto you the whole armor of God, that ye may be able to withstand in the evil day, and having done all, to stand.

Ephesians 6: 12-13

ABOUT THE AUTHOR

Joyce Swann homeschooled her ten children from the first grade through master's degrees. She is a well-known author and speaker on the subject of homeschooling. For nearly a decade she was a popular columnist for *Practical Homeschooling* Magazine. She now blogs regularly on parenting, homeschooling, and Christian lifestyle issues.

Joyce has co-authored two other novels, *The Fourth Kingdom* and *The Twelfth Juror,* both of which were published in 2010. Her personal story of her experiences raising and educating her family is chronicled in *Looking Backward: My Twenty-Five Years as a Homeschooling Mother,* published in February of 2011. She is also the author of two children's books, *Tales of Pig Isle* and *The McAloons*, which began as stories that she told to entertain her grandchildren.

Joyce and her husband John live in Anthony, New Mexico, in the same house where they raised their family.

Made in the USA
Lexington, KY
30 January 2013